D0474011

"You kissed me!" she
accused him angrily.

"Yes," he nodded. "Isn't it the classic way
of waking a lady? You've been so far
under for the last thirty kilometers it was a
choice between assault and battery,
yelling in your ear, or the pleasurable
method I used."

"Pleasurable?" she echoed. "To kiss me?"
She pushed herself upright on the
seat—a movement that brought her close
to Karl.

"Such a fuss about a spur-of-the-moment
kiss," he murmured, and with studied
deliberation took her mouth again.
"There are kisses and kisses, didn't you
know?"

When she got out and watched him drive
away, Juliet was trembling, close to tears.
Of anger? Shame? Or regret? All of
them formed a tangle of emotions she
couldn't analyze. . . .

OTHER
Harlequin Romances
by JANE ARBOR

832—NO SILVER SPOON
858—MY SURGEON NEIGHBOUR
887—LAKE OF SHADOWS
919—DEAR INTRUDER
950—KINGFISHER TIDE
1000—A GIRL NAMED SMITH
1043—HIGH MASTER OF CLERE
1108—SUMMER EVERY DAY
1157—YESTERDAY'S MAGIC
1182—GOLDEN APPLE ISLAND
1277—STRANGER'S TRESPASS
1336—THE CYPRESS GARDEN
1406—WALK INTO THE WIND
1443—THE FEATHERED SHAFT
1480—THE LINDEN LEAF
1544—THE OTHER MISS DONNE
1582—WILDFIRE QUEST
1665—THE FLOWER ON THE ROCK
1740—ROMAN SUMMER
1789—THE VELVET SPUR
1832—MEET THE SUN HALFWAY
1896—THE WIDE FIELDS OF HOME
1963—SMOKE INTO FLAME
2033—TREE OF PARADISE
2066—TWO PINS IN A FOUNTAIN
2108—A GROWING MOON

Many of these titles are available at your local bookseller
or through the Harlequin Reader Service.

For a free catalogue listing all available Harlequin Romances,
send your name and address to:

HARLEQUIN READER SERVICE,
M.P.O. Box 707, Niagara Falls, N.Y. 14302
Canadian address: Stratford, Ontario, Canada N5A 6W2

or use coupon at back of book.

Return to Silbersee

by

JANE ARBOR

Harlequin Books

TORONTO • LONDON • NEW YORK • AMSTERDAM
SYDNEY • HAMBURG • PARIS

Original hardcover edition published in 1978
by Mills & Boon Limited

ISBN 0-373-02231-X

Harlequin edition published January 1979

Copyright © 1978 by Jane Arbor.
Philippine copyright 1978. Australian copyright 1978.

All rights reserved. Except for use in any review, the reproduction or utilization
of this work in whole or in part in any form by any electronic, mechanical or
other means, now known or hereafter invented, including xerography,
photocopying and recording, or in any information storage or retrieval system,
is forbidden without the permission of the publisher. All the characters in this
book have no existence outside the imagination of the author and have no
relation whatsoever to anyone bearing the same name or names. They are not
even distantly inspired by any individual known or unknown to the author, and
all the incidents are pure invention.

The Harlequin trademark, consisting of the word HARLEQUIN and the
portrayal of a Harlequin, is registered in the United States Patent
Office and the Canada Trade Marks Office.

Printed in Canada

CHAPTER ONE

ON either side of the downward road from the snow-line the scene contradicted itself.

Under the thick canopy of the forest trees the soil was dark, dry and loamy; where the country opened out the hedges were massed white with blackthorn blossom, though snow still lay in the field furrows and on the roofs of lonely farmsteads; there was real warmth in the sunshine, but the wind had a knife-edge. As usual, the hand of Bavaria's winter was still holding fast to the reluctant fingers of its spring.

Juliet drove slowly, watching for a sheltered spot where she could pull in and park and eat her packed lunch with the car door open to the sun. At last she found one—a small roadside clearing which led back to a forest ride. She passed it at first, then backed on to it and got out to see if perhaps she could picnic outside.

There was no view, except across the road to fields already under the plough, but the wind was only a howling behind the trees and the calm air was almost balmy. She threw back the hood of her anorak and was standing with her face lifted to the sun when another car passed on the road, slowed a hundred or so metres ahead, then backed down as she had done in her own car.

She frowned, annoyed at the prospect of sharing her little well-found spot with anyone. This was a by-road; her triangle of springy turf wasn't marked by authority as a layby for tourists; there were plenty of finer beauty spots higher up the Pass and lower down, near the Lake, and there really was no reason why——!

She stood her ground as the driver drew level with her and stopped. Perhaps, she hoped, he only wanted to ask his way. But apparently not, for he was getting out, slamming his door and peeling off his gauntlets as if he had arrived to a welcome at his journey's end.

Which was absurd. Since this out-of-the-way neck of the woods couldn't possibly be anywhere where he meant to finish up, Juliet made her look at him cool and uninviting.

He was blond, tall, a virile giant of a man, an easy-muscled golden-skinned type with, she had to allow, at least a vestige of good manners in his slight bow as he asked,

'Stretching your legs after a long drive, Fräulein? D'you mind if I do the same?'

She questioned, 'Here? Of course not. But you could have found some places with better views further back, I'd have thought.'

He stood, legs apart, hands on the hips of his leather jerkin, and lifted one shoulder in a shrug.

'Perhaps,' he agreed. 'But after I had passed, I thought I rather liked what I had seen here, so I came back.'

Though the words were innocuous, there was no mistaking the practised flattery of the look which accompanied them, and which Juliet deliberately ignored by continuing, 'There's some fine scenery too as one drops down to the Silbersee. But perhaps that isn't your road?'

'Is it yours?'

'Yes—eventually.' (If he expected they would make

a caravanserai of two cars when they moved on, then he had better think again!)

He said, 'Ah well, I'm on my way to Munich— *eventually*. Or rather, returning there from across the Austrian border.'

'But this isn't the main road for Munich,' Juliet pointed out.

'No, but I made a detour up to Innsgort to judge the last of the skiing prospects. You've been up there yourself?'

She nodded. 'I had one day. I stayed overnight.'

His glance went to her car, apparently noting that no skis were strapped to it nor thrusting from its boot. 'No gear?'

'I don't bring it down. I left it up there,' she said shortly, feeling no need to enlarge on why it wasn't with her this time.

'And now?'

'I stopped here to picnic before going on.'

'Alone?'

'I like picnicking alone.'

He laughed. 'The snub direct! Or may I hope you are merely being tactful about telling me that you haven't brought enough Knackwurst or Pretzels to share?' When she did not reply and turned back to her car, he went on,

'Very well. Snub taken, and though it's a free country and I could sit in the offing until you took pity on me and threw me a crust, I won't embarrass you so far. Enjoy your lone sausage, Fräulein!' But as he got into his own car he looked over his shoulder. 'But you are not a Fräulein, are you? For all your good German, you are not one of us?'

'No. I'm English.'

He took his seat and handled the steering-wheel.
'Ah, that bears it out,' he murmured.

'Bears out what?' she questioned, seeking an opening for a retort which would wither him.

'The popular theory we have that all the English are
born with only half a heart,' he claimed coolly, and to
judge by his carelessly sketched salute, he was singu-
larly unwithered as he drove away.

Cheated of her retort but glad he seemed to have
realised that she wasn't fair game for an arrogant take-
over, Juliet unwrapped the napkin around her food,
which wasn't sausage, but blue cheese and rye bread,
a slice of rich *Torte* and an outsize orange, put up for
her by the Innsgort hotel. She thought about the
stranger.

Not easy to place. Big, powerful car. Informal but
good clothes, carelessly worn. Cultured voice. An
assurance amounting almost to conceit. Businessman?
Professional? Playboy? Anyway, as much of an oppor-
tunist as the next man, if he could claim to have been
attracted by the sight of her very ordinary figure,
anoraked and sturdily booted against the cold, long
dark hair lifted and tangled by the wind, normally fair
skin stung to a glow and, in all probability, the tip of
her undistinguished nose unbecomingly red.

And yet, for all his easy assumption that lone-girl-
in-car-making-unforced-stop-by-wayside added up to
invitation-to-any-male-happening-along, somehow she
was left with the impression that *if* they had met in
the way of business or socially, she wouldn't have dismissed him as a mere Lochinvar with ideas above his
station. She might even have found him attractive ...

Deliberately she broke off her thought there and
spread butter on her *Roggenbrot* with a generous hand.

He was on his way to Munich now, his abortive attempt to pick her up half forgotten and behind him, while she had other problems ever present and ahead of her, in which the silly encounter had no place.

She thought about yesterday—her last of skiing on the Innsgort slopes. Not because the season was over —Innsgort kept good snow conditions through the blackthorn winter of late April and sometimes into May—but because, between now and when she left *Rutgen-ober-Silbersee*, she would not be going to Innsgort again. That was why she had sold her skiing gear before coming down this time.

She was going to hate leaving the Silbersee, the silver lake that was more often green and blue and, under storm, a drab grey, and only a true gleaming silver by moonlight. Which was how she had first seen it herself, arriving by taxi from Gutbach, the nearest railway station—how long ago now? A few months short of three years, in a wild autumn with the threat of a cruel winter, the fullness of which, that time, she had not stayed long enough to experience.

And now, sitting here in a forest clearing, she was conning over the harsh economics which were forcing her back to England a second time. Not, actually, her own problem, those economics, but with enough chain reaction to change a pattern of work and living which, since her return to the Lake, she had enjoyed.

She prolonged her picnic for more than an hour, scattering the crumbs of her meal for the birds before she left to drive the rest of her way home.

In late April the sun went behind the Volksspitze, the highest peak of the Frohnbergs, by mid-afternoon, and she was going to be glad to gain the warmth of the Wood-carving School chalet—the long, one-storeyed building facing the lake, at one end of which she had her quarters.

That first time she had written back to England that Rutgen was 'oh, so quaint and terribly Brothers Grimm', but the longer she had seen and lived in it since, the more she was captivated by the charm of its hamlet-scatter of small houses, almost all with their façades to the lake, except those which looked at each other across the tiny village square; its dark backcloth of immemorial forest trees; the slender-spired church with its tinny-sounding Glockenspiel and its high-perched Schloss, turreted and grey and brooding by day, but in its present guise as an hotel, fairyland arc-lighted by night.

The school building was wholly of wood, with an openwork carved balcony running its full length, and its title-legend *Die Schule des Schnitzarbeits* in a crescent of carved old German lettering above its central entrance door.

Juliet's own quarters—a living-room, a bedroom, kitchen and bathroom—had the same rich smell of cedar as had the school workshops. And it had a tiny terraced garden, from which a short flight of wooden steps led down to the lake-edge. She had promised herself a lot of pottering in that garden—come the summer she wouldn't now see.

This was the end of the winter work season, and there would have been no one in the shops except perhaps old Wilhelm Konstat, her right-hand man, that day. After opening up the living-room stove to a glow, she had switched on the kettle and was splitting some muffins for toasting for her tea, when the telephone rang. The automatic kettle switched itself off as she lifted the receiver to a call from the Baronin, the widowed owner of the Schloss von Boden, the castle home of generations of von Bodens until the new-poor Baroness Magda von Boden had opened and run it herself as a high-class guesthouse some ten years earlier. She was still, as always, 'lady of the manor' to the tenants of her late husband's vast wooded estate, and Juliet felt privileged to know herself to be one of the few people, apart from her men of business, to whom the Baronin had confided the financial difficulties forced upon her by her own increasing age and the headlong race of costs which couldn't be halted. In her seventieth year the gallant Baroness was a tired woman and one whose future, but for the drastic moves to which circumstances had driven her, looked bleak indeed.

'Julie?' The Baronin always used the German form of Juliet's name. 'Oh, you are there? I thought you mightn't yet be back from Innsgort. I rang because— look, dear, I haven't much time, for he is on his way now. Left the Schloss a few minutes ago. Looking round some of the tenancies, including the School. He isn't with you already, by the way?'

Knowing coherence to be no strong point of her friend's when she was in a hurry or agitated, Juliet said patiently, 'No, no one has called here since I got in. But who is "he"?'

There was so long a pause that the Baronin might not have heard the question. At last she said, 'This you won't understand and probably won't like. But it's Herr Adler—Karl Adler, the Chairman and Chief Director of Adler Classics. Gerhard's half-brother, whom Gerhard never let either of us meet, though when Gerhard died and I was abroad for a month at the time, I understand he came to the funeral. And now he—that is, the Adler Group are doing this deal for my standing timber, and he wanted, he said, to make a personal and informal survey of the estate. He arrived, right out of the blue, just this afternoon.'

On a long breath of surprise, Juliet said, 'You're right. I don't understand, and it *is* a bit of a shock. But why Karl Adler? What has his firm to do with your sale? Your solicitors have been negotiating with Hartung Gesellschaft of Hanover, haven't they?'

'Yes. But Hartung have fallen to a lightning take-over by Adler. I've known of it for a week. But I saw the whole thing being done at boardroom level—signatures on the dotted line, and all that. I didn't sup-pose there would be any personal contacts necessary. Even with me, and still less with you. You understand, Julie? I told him about you, of course——'

'*All* about me?' questioned Juliet heavily.

'Oh no. Only how you came originally to take a course under Gerhard, and went back to teaching han-dicrafts in an English school. And how, when he died fifteen months or so later, I persuaded you to come back and run the management side of the School. Nothing at all about Gerhard and you, Julie. I assure you, *nothing*.'

'Well, thank you,' Juliet said. 'At least I'm prepared, if Gerhard has to be mentioned. But there's something I don't understand. You are selling a lot of your stand-ing timber. Right? But since neither Hartung nor Adler are buying the *estate*, what interest can Herr Adler have in your tenants' holdings?'

'Yes, well, that's——' But at an interjection from Juliet the Baronin paused. 'What is it, dear? Has he arrived?'

'I think so. I heard a car.'

'Well, ring me, won't you, when he has gone?'

'Yes.' Juliet replaced the receiver and went to the door which gave straight into the living-room. Against the deepening twilight the man on the threshold was at first only in silhouette. Then he offered his hand. 'Fräulein Harmon? I am Karl Adler. May I come in?' he said. And came in.

Her recognition of him was of course instant though incredulous. *That* man, her noontime brash gallant, had been on his way to Munich and had had time to waste. He wasn't a self-made tycoon, reputed to have made a million from mass-produced furniture design before reaching his mid-thirties; the half-brother of dead Gerhard Minden, both of them handling the same raw material—wood, but one of them a big-business Colossus and the other an individual, dedicated craftsman.

Or was he? If he were Karl Adler, and he said he was, then he had to be also her stranger of the morning. For he was the same virile hunk of man, bearing the same assuredness of a welcome until—— Why had his obvious recognition of her suddenly turned to a cold stare, disconcerting in its intensity and utterly chilling in its appraisal? This morning he had wanted to know her, however flirtatiously; tonight his look seemed to convey that there was nothing he wanted less. She also had the impression that his polite 'May I come in?' before he recognised her had been more of an order than a request. He had *meant* to come into Juliet Harmon's house, invited or not, and he intended censure and blame of her when he arrived. What could he know?

As calmly as she could she moved back from him

and went to sit by the stove, pointing him to another chair, which he took.

She said levelly, 'We met this morning by coincidence, didn't we, Herr Adler? Without either of us knowing who the other was?'

He nodded. 'Though you must know I've heard of you before—in none too favourable terms?'

'Really?' Though his look had conveyed it, Juliet had to conceal her shock. Had the Baronin lied then that she hadn't gossiped to him? Surely not? But if not Magda von Boden, then who? She took refuge in counter-attack.

'And you must know that I've heard about *you*— from Gerhard, your half-brother, whom you refused to see or help, even when his doctors had given him an indefinitely short time to live!'

'I didn't refuse to see him. Our estrangement was mutual and of years' long standing—ever since, in fact, my mother separated from Gerhard's father and took me with her, the four of us never meeting again, as you probably know.'

Juliet said, 'I do know. Also that it was by no fault of mine that you didn't see Gerhard before he died. I wrote you a letter——'

'I never received one.'

'No. When I told Gerhard what I had done, he made me destroy it. But then, without his knowing, I came to your offices in Munich; sent in my name to you, only to be told that you saw no one without their stating their business.'

'Reasonable, surely? I'm a busy man, and at that date I had never heard of you.'

'No, though I'd have thought you could bend a rule, considering I had said my business was personal.'

'My dear girl!' Karl Adler laughed shortly. 'You evidently don't realise the extent to which cranks and spongers regard "personal" as a kind of talisman for gaining sympathy for their woes. You could have mentioned Gerhard's name and sent my secretary to me again.'

Juliet drew herself up. 'And I would *not* mention his name. If your attitude to him was the same as his towards you, it would have got me no further. And what was more, if you couldn't accept that I *had* business with you that *was* personal——'

'——You were damned if you were going on your knees to plead with me, or alternatively, sit up and beg? Was that it?'

'More or less.'

He tilted his head and regarded her judicially. 'And isn't there a word for that attitude? Known, isn't it, as cutting off your nose to spite your face?'

She flushed. 'Yes. Perhaps.'

'And because of it I never did see Gerhard before he died.'

'Not just because of that. You knew where he was, what he was doing!' she accused.

'And he knew where I was, and what I was doing. He had only to write or pick up the phone, if he had wanted to make contact.'

'I've told you, he didn't want to. And the only gesture you ever made towards *him* was to attend his funeral!'

'Ah, you heard about that? But you weren't present yourself, were you?'

'No,' she snapped. 'I'd gone back to England over a year earlier.'

'Taking with you any guilt you may have had in

relation to Gerhard, or effectually sloughing it off—
that is, if you had ever had any?'

Her voice dangerously quiet, 'And what do you
mean by that, Herr Adler?'

Equally quietly, 'I think you know, Fräulein—er—
Miss Juliet Harmon, whose name and connection with
Gerhard I first learned when I came to his funeral.'

'Of which I didn't hear until after it was over. And
learned from whom, please?'

He shrugged. 'From the locals. No one in particular.
I stayed around for a few days, and their sympathy for
Gerhard needed to tell the whole story.'

'And you learned—what?'

'The truth as they saw it, and I think they saw it
straight. That you came here as Gerhard's student in
wood-carving; that he fell deeply in love with you;
asked you to marry him, being frank about the spinal
illness which would give him, at most, only a year or
two more to live, and you refused, though he asked
you, begged you over and over again. You admitted
there was no other man for you, that you had no other
romantic ties at all, and as your village saw it, you had
little to lose in a compassion for Gerhard which could
only ask a very short term of you—a term of companionship and care of him which, in these good folks'
opinion, shouldn't have cost you too much.'

'But companionship wasn't what Gerhard was asking of me. He wanted—and deserved—a wife, and that
I couldn't make him. I didn't love him,' Juliet said.

'Though, loving *you* enough, don't you think he
might have settled for less?' Karl Adler countered.

Her chin went up. 'He declared he could, but I
daren't take him at his word for his own sake. I——'
She paused, doubting if she could convey to this self-

appointed judge her deepest conviction that the only reason for marriage should be the shouted *Yes* of love on both sides—and decided against trying. She went on, 'That is, I dared not humiliate him by marrying him for pity. However short the marriage was, it wouldn't have been enough. I was convinced of that.'

'And so I failed him until it was too late. But you failed him living, knowing what you could do for him, and refusing. Which of us, would you say, should have the worse conscience then?'

'Have I blamed you, as you've seen fit to blame me?' she retorted. 'And, short of marrying him, I did all I could. I tried to see you about him, with no result. I offered, when my course was finished, to stay on for a while as his friend——'

Karl Adler looked about him. 'Here? You lived with him here?'

Her grasp on the arms of her chair tightened convulsively, showing her knuckles white. '*Here?* With him? I was lodging with some people named Konstat nearby!'

'And "as his friend"? Could one read into that perhaps the "good friend" of journalistic jargon or the "little friend" as our neighbours the French put it? You wouldn't let him do you the honour of marrying you, but you were willing to compromise, as long as you weren't tied down? For as long as it suited you, you would have stayed as his——'

But at that Juliet's pent anger propelled her forward, out of her chair and in a longer stride than she thought she could make, she faced him, close above him, her furious eyes levelling with his, her right hand raised ... ready.

He caught at her wrist in time, twisted it and flung

her hand from him. 'Guttersnipe tactics, hm? Hitting out when you've either no case or haven't control enough to plead it?' he taunted. 'You know, I'd advise you to go back to your chair and count ten before you speak again.'

'Not—not until you've apologised for——'

'For drawing the rather obvious inference from your own words?' He shook his head. 'No call for apology there. *I* could claim that you tempted me to it, and we'd need an appeal court to judge the issue between us. So I suggest we forget it. I've belatedly made the acquaintance of Miss Juliet Harmon and she, much against her will, has met me. That we did it this morning in a slightly less hostile vein is neither here nor there, and as I came primarily to talk business with Miss Harmon, would she allow me to get on with it now?'

Forget it! Shrugging off one of the worst insults a man could throw at a woman, and suggesting she should 'forget it'! It showed he wasn't convinced that she hadn't been prepared to be Gerhard's mistress, and if he had been someone whose faith and good opinion she valued deeply, she couldn't have felt more sickened. Yet why should she care what this man thought of her? What was he, after all? A shape, a name; self-introduced this morning and having the utter gall to play judge and jury tonight. What *she* had to forget—and could—was that for even an instant's thought she had debated his male attraction ...

With all the dignity she could muster she returned to her seat. 'Well?' she said. 'Your business? What is it?'

'This,' he said. 'I take it that Baronin von Boden

phoned you after I had left the Schloss? She said she was going to.'

'She did.'

'And told you of the circumstances which brought me here?'

'About your takeover of the Hartung Group, yes. No details of why you came today.'

'Yes, well, that was a personal whim.' He paused. 'Not entirely unconnected, I admit, with an interest in how Gerhard's School had fared since his death.'

'Really? Well, it has "fared" so far, as you see. You expected to find me here, so you'll have heard from the Baronin that, at her request, I came back to manage its affairs some months ago, taking over your half-brother's tenancy of the building and occupying his quarters.' (If Magda von Boden hadn't told him that her decision to give up the hotel was the threat which must also close the School, then let him find out that for himself!) At this stage Juliet herself wasn't going to admit to the dependence on the hotel guests of Gerhard's skilled handcraftsmen for the sale of their winter's work; nor to the hotel's summer employment of them as waiters and kitchenmen and porters. It was a time-honoured cycle of Rutgen's livelihood that was about to be broken through no one's fault, least of all the Baronin's or Juliet's own. But no doubt Mr Big Business opposite could convince himself that she had failed Gerhard in this direction too. She would volunteer nothing.

He was saying now, 'Ah, your tenancy. That's what concerns me. How long has it now to run?'

'About two more years.'

'Only two? So no problem. You will have very little to lose.'

Juliet pondered this, frowning. 'To lose? By what?'

'By Adler Classics' compensating you and your neighbours for your loss of tenancy when we build a sawmill on this stretch of the lake-shore.'

'A—a *sawmill*?' Juliet's echo was shrill. 'On the Silbersee? You can't be serious? It would be a desecration!'

'But a very necessary adjunct to a purchase of standing timber. Or do you suggest we put ropes round the lumber and lug it by oxenpower to our next nearest sawmill plant, when we've an ideal site for one here?'

'But you'd be destroying the homes of a dozen families, not to mention this place which had all Gerhard Minden's devotion and all his work!'

'And providing work and a future for a multiplication of a dozen families. Also housing elsewhere on the estate, as we should have to build accommodation for the lumbermen we'd be importing, and a few more cottages for you displaced persons shouldn't tax us too much.'

'A select line in concrete boxes, set end to end?' Juliet scorned. His use of 'you' had told her that he knew nothing of her plan to leave, and the fragments of a ruse began to merge in her mind.

He shook his head. 'I doubt if we'll use either brick or concrete when wood is our trade, and we'll have so much of it at our disposal. No, I hereby pledge that your new houses shall be of wood, and if your alleged concern for the tradition of Gerhard's work is revolted at running his School anywhere than here, I daresay your wood-carvers and your pupils could turn their skilled hands to dealing with wood on a wider scale. With us.'

'As lumbermen or builders? They wouldn't thank

you, believe me! They *choose* wood and mould it and fashion it by hand. They don't take a hatchet to it and chop it up into two-by-fours. And they are able to sell what they make because, believe it or not, there are still people who value beautiful, hand-made things to live with!'

'Don't we all, when we can afford them? Though most of us don't therefore choose to sit on the floor rather than use modern chairs and tables for comfort and convenience. But tell me, Miss Harmon, *who*, in heaven's name, taught you to regard some piece of furniture that's been turned by machine as an intrinsically nasty thing?'

'I never said that it was!' she retorted to the deceptive mildness of the question. 'I only pointed out that my craftsmen—Gerhard's—couldn't and wouldn't switch jobs at your say-so, just like that.'

She was awarded Karl Adler's tolerant nod. 'That's better,' he murmured. 'I had the impression you meant to be beastly to the necessity of two-by-fours. And if you insist that only small is beautiful, we shall really have to educate you by taking you round one of our plants and demonstrating that a lot of Adler Classics are likely to become the treasured antiques of a hundred or so years hence. We happen, you see,' he added in sure mimicry of her own tone and words, 'to "fashion" our pieces with quality in mind.'

To which she longed to murmur back an ironic, 'Thank you. I'm sure I should be edified. Though too bad, isn't it, that I shan't be here?' But such triumph was out, now that, in the last few caustic minutes, her under-mind had pieced together its resolve. So she made no reply, and he rose to leave with a 'Well, as long as you understand the position——' Then she asked,

'Were you thinking of seeing the other affected tenants before you go back to Munich as, this morning, you said you meant to?'

One corner of his mouth lifted, suggesting the ghost of a smile.

'Ah, this morning was a world away,' he said. 'And my plans were fluid. I may see one or two of these others on my way back to the Schloss, but as I am staying there for a few days, I can afford to take my time.'

Surprised, Juliet said sharply, 'I didn't know the Baronin was taking any more guests.'

'No. A pity. But she has made a gracious exception for me.'

'And supposing'—Juliet had her rapier ready—'supposing they, or even some of them, won't agree to abandon their tenancies?'

His shrug made light of the suggestion. 'I think there's no fear of that. We shan't stint on our compensation. It will be generous.'

'But if even only one held out, what then?'

'It might hold up the project for a while, but we'd have ways of dealing with that.'

She went with him to the door and opened it. Outside the twilight had deepened and a new moon was cradled in the sky above the lake. She held out her hand and he took it.

'Then perhaps you had better begin to look into those ways,' she said. 'Because I, for one, am not abandoning my tenancy for any amount of compensation you like to offer. I have the right to hold it for nearly two years, and I'm doing just that!'

He looked down at her, his grasp on her hand tightening until she could have cried out at the pressure on its bones. No parting handshake that, but a threat.

He said, almost musing to himself, 'So—fangs and claws, as well as only half a heart! My half-brother was lucky after all—he didn't know what he missed,' and released her hand and went out.

When she had shut the door on him, Juliet ran back to the telephone. Even if he were driving straight back to the Schloss, she could gain the Baronin's ear before he got there. She dialled with a shaking finger. 'Magda?'

'Yes, Julie, here. You've seen Herr Adler? What happened?'

'Listen, Magda. I haven't much time. He may be there with you at any minute, and I hear you are putting him up. Meanwhile, I gather you hadn't told him that I was on the point of leaving, or as soon as you closed the hotel?'

There was a small silence. Then the Baronin hesitated. 'No. No, I'm sure I didn't. I didn't get so far in telling him about you. Or did I——? No, I don't think I did. Why?'

'Well, I'm convinced you didn't, for he gave no sign of knowing it. And now you mustn't tell him. Please, Magda, must *not*! For now it wouldn't be true of me. I've changed my mind, and I'm staying!'

CHAPTER TWO

IF there were one trait of Magda von Boden's for which Juliet was grateful, it was her ability to let people make their own decisions. Faced by a stand or a conviction she would listen, comment or question. But she rarely persuaded for or against. She allowed others to act by their own standards, however mistaken she might consider them herself.

It had been so when Juliet had confided her dilemma in refusing Gerhard's proposal; whether or no the Baronin thought she lacked compassion, she hadn't presumed to judge her for it. And it had been the same when Juliet had announced her lightning face-about in the matter of her staying on in defence of the School's continuance of its tenancy. She hadn't even reminded Juliet of her previous despair that without its link with the hotel, it couldn't carry on. Over the telephone she had sounded glad at Juliet's change of heart, but had been content to say, 'Well I'm sure I can allow you to know best, dear,' in several different ways in answer to Juliet's disjointed account of her reasons, still somewhat confused in her mind, though her need to stay was clear enough. It would baulk Karl holier-than-thou Adler in his tracks!

When she had rung off Juliet had gone through to the deserted workshops and looked at the familiar benches, empty now of their tools at the end of the season, the chisels and files wrapped in oiled cloth and tidied away into drawers, the planes and soldering-irons covered by hoods, the glues and the polishes returned to store.

Beyond the main workroom were a cupboard and a miniature counter where Frau Konstat and other workers' wives served morning coffee, beer and snacks on a voluntary rota. Beyond was Gerhard's office where Juliet now worked, and beyond that again was the stockroom, piled now with the winter season's products—the salad bowls and servers, the paper-knives, the primal doll and animal shapes, the trays, the chessmen, the trinket boxes, all ready for sale to a hitherto eager and wealthy clientèle. And everywhere was that heady aroma of warm wood and linseed oil and fresh shavings that was as all-pervading as incense in a church; a distillation of perfume like no other Juliet knew.

Last night she had stood in the workroom wrapped in the euphoria of her decision to stand by the School whatever happened, telling herself, 'If ever it could be said that I owed Gerhard anything, I owe him this.' But by the light of a grey April morning ideals had to face realities and didn't care much for what they saw.

With no work for them at the hotel, she would have to bring her team back into the shops and find a different sales outlet for their produce, beginning with the stockpile that needed moving now. But where to look for sales? The School had never needed to employ salesmen going round with samples, and in any case, could not afford them. But now there would have to be a sales force—of one. The stark truth forced itself upon her—it was she who would have to spend part of her time bearding the fancy goods wholesalers of Munich and even further afield, tramping up and down their unfriendly stairs and steeling herself against the rebuffs she was bound to get.

But she *would* carry on. She *would* sell the stuff. She

would throw that man's sneer of 'small is beautiful'
back in his teeth! And though he wasn't likely to want
to meet her again, she almost wished he would. Per-
verse though she might be, she had actually enjoyed
last night's encounter—especially winning. Her hand
was still tender from his vice-like grip on it which had
betrayed his anger. Round One. And any time he
chose for Round Two—if he did—couldn't be soon
enough for her. She had never been so dynamically
challenged by a man in her life. By comparison with
Gerhard and the wearing-down means by which he had
tried to impose his will upon her, she suspected that
Karl Adler's methods with an opponent would have
the bright cutting edge of cold steel. He had probably
made his tycoon's way in the world just so. But why
was she comparing him with Gerhard at all? They
weren't even related, except by their respective parents' marriage to each other. And Gerhard had wanted
to marry her. Futile to draw parallels at all ...

Spoiling for action, she decided to walk down to Wilhelm Konstat's chalet to sound him out on her decision
to stay and to find out whether Karl Adler had called
on him last night. He had not, it seemed, but Wilhelm
had it on the Lake grapevine that he had called on two
others of the Baronin's shore tenants and had named
his terms.

'Who were they?' Juliet asked. Wilhelm told her.
'But they didn't agree?' she said.

'Hmm,' said Wilhelm. He had no word of English
and had picked up none from her, and most of her
fluent German which Karl Adler had condescended to
term 'good' she had learned from him and recognised
his 'Hmm' as his bid for time before making an
answer.

Her pulse quickened. Surely they weren't going to let her down—go over to the enemy without a fight? 'They didn't agree—*did* they?' she pressed.

Wilhelm made up his mind. 'They didn't say Yes and they didn't say No to him. Not for them to say either, was it? The Herr wants to build his sawmill. He was telling them that, and that he will pay them to move out of their houses to make room for it.'

'But they don't have to move!' Juliet protested.

'They have to, if the Baronin has agreed to rent the land to the Herr,' Wilhelm maintained.

'Even the Baronin can't turn us out while our properties still have leases to run,' Juliet declared desperately. 'Herr Adler wants to pull down the School too. He came to see me last night, and I told him I refused to move. And you and the others should do the same. Then he can't——' She broke off awkwardly at the old man's questioning glance. 'Yes, I know,' she admitted, reading its meaning, 'I thought we'd have to close the School when the hotel closes. But I've decided to stay on after all. We'll have to find some other outlets for selling our stuff, and to keep people at work, but there's no reason why we shouldn't produce all summer as well as winter. Anyway, we've probably had it too easy, being able to sell all we could make to the tourists at the hotel, and it's time we began to strike *out*.'

'Hmm,' said Wilhelm again. And then, 'You hadn't told *me* about this.'

'I'm telling you now. I only decided last night, quite suddenly.'

'To fight the Herr and his sawmill?' Wilhelm queried shrewdly.

Juliet nodded. 'We can't stop him felling as much timber as the Baronin lets him have. But we can make him find somewhere else for his sawmill, if we all refuse to move.'

'Though there are those on the shore who might welcome his money to get themselves a house in Gutbach or Stronberg, where there'd be work in plenty,' Wilhelm demurred.

'And others who would break their hearts if they had to leave the Lake,' Juliet countered. 'What about Grandpa Weisskop, who would be willing to retire if we'd closed the School, but who has never done anything but wood-carving all his life? Or Helmut Jäger —what about him? He couldn't find work in Gutbach that he could do.'

'*Ach*, blind Helmut,' Wilhelm mused compassionately. 'He must use his hands for eyes, or be idle, as we know. And so, Fräulein, you would have me say No to the Herr, even though the Baronin has told him Yes? You do not like him, I take it, Fräulein?'

'It is mutual. He made it very clear he didn't like *me*,' Juliet admitted frankly. 'Mostly, I think from what he heard about me when he came to Herr Minden's funeral.'

'Yes, that,' said Wilhelm. 'Knowing, as we did, that Gerhard Minden had wanted to marry you, perhaps we were too bitter to speak kindly of you then. But we know you now, and you can be very sure that Herr Adler will hear nothing but praise of you if he should ask us how we regard you since you came back to the Lake.'

It was a promise which, kindly as it was meant, set all Juliet's hackles of pride abristle. Depend on her friends' championship to gain favour with Karl Adler she would *not*! But she managed a wry smile for Wilhelm.

'I doubt if anything you say will convince him that I am nice to know. I'd guess that prejudice is his middle name. Meanwhile, all I ask is that you should consider giving him a very firm No when he——'

'When he——?'

The echo had come from behind her, where she and Wilhelm stood, just inside his living-room, the outside door ajar. The voice was that of Karl Adler, who had come up the house path unheard. Juliet turned, startled to an undignified, 'Oh!'

His cool glance raked her. 'Out early, canvassing the vote? How are you doing so far? Gaining support, or are the "Don't Knows" getting you down?' He turned to Wilhelm, offering a hand. 'We've met before, haven't we? You remember me?'

'Yes, indeed, Herr Adler. You were present at Herr Minden's funeral.'

'That's right. At a time when we hadn't the pleasure of Fräulein Harmon's company. As, while we talk business, if she will forgive us, we could dispense with it now.' Though a faint smile accompanied the words, the hint was so blatant that Juliet almost gasped. Ignoring it, she said to Wilhelm, 'Will you come over to the School this evening? I'd like to go through the stock with you.' Then, with a heavily emphasised, '*Bitte*, Herr Adler,' she swept past him through the open door.

He came after her. 'May I hope to find you at home later in the morning?' he asked.

'I couldn't say, though I shall probably be there,' she said.

'I hope you will try to be.' That was all. He went back to Wilhelm with an air of having issued an order which would be obeyed.

Seething, Juliet walked back home. The clouds had broken and the sun had come out, dimpling the lake surface with blue and green lights. Being free on such a day, she would probably have packed a lunch, taken a book and gone walking in the woods, and she was sorely tempted, for more than one reason, to do just that today. But if she were going to reorganise things at the School, there was work to do, and though there would be some satisfaction in bilking the enemy, there would be more in standing her ground and facing him. Besides, she was feeling again the tingle of challenge which had enjoyed their crossing of swords last night. In her present mood, if he weren't there like a thorn under a fingernail, she would have to invent him. She was spoiling for a fight.

Deciding on a simple midday meal of thick soup and fruit, she checked that she had bone stock in the refrigerator, and she soaked dried peas to add to cold carrots and potatoes for a purée. Then, taking a note-pad and a street map of Munich, she went through a trades directory in search of wholesalers and retailers of fancy goods in the city. She wasn't sorry that Karl Adler should find her at work on this when he arrived a couple of hours later. She would have liked to blind him with statistics of the School's success, or at least to impress him with the fact of its importance to the Lake, and the need for *someone* to work at its affairs.

But to her chagrin, he showed no curiosity as to what she was doing. Nor did he report on his interview with Wilhelm or with whomever he had called to see. He came, he said, to invite her to lunch with him and the

Baronin in the hotel dining-room. 'A *business* luncheon,' he emphasised.

An olive-branch? Surely not. Then a trap? 'Thank you,' she said stiffly, 'but I've work to do, and I've already planned my luncheon.'

'Then you refuse? That's a pity. I know the Baronin hoped you would join us.' His tone was formal, detached, indifferent.

Juliet looked him squarely in the eyes. 'You know, I would doubt that,' she said.

'Really? Why? I understood that she and you were great friends?'

'And so we are. And it's because I think she is as fond of me as I am of her that I say I doubt if she would really welcome being a witness to the kind of hostility you showed for me last night. It would vex her and at the very least, embarrass her. So thank you, no. I won't lunch.'

At that he laughed, disconcerting her. 'My dear girl,' he expostulated, 'do you suppose I eat and drink my minor controversies and regurgitate them at the very next opportunity——?'

'To me, the differences between us hardly rank as "minor",' Juliet cut in.

'Even so, you should be capable of rising above them from time to time, I'd have thought. High enough, any way, to enable you to accept a mere luncheon date. Besides, if you're afraid I might turn savage across the table, I assure you I rarely allow wrath to spoil for me a well-chosen menu and a mellow wine. Again, if you're still in doubt of my manners, on this occasion you have the Baronin as a buffer state between us, haven't you?'

'Though I'd prefer not to use her as a buffer state, if you don't mind.'

'You won't have to. I don't brawl in public. Though how do you know she wouldn't enjoy acting as peace-maker, if the need arose?' he taunted. 'So will you come?'

His derision, his assumption that she had something to fear from him decided her. If she continued to re-fuse, he would see it as weakness, and that she could *not* tolerate! But feeling that a bland acceptance would choke her, after a moment's hesitation she evaded it with a glance down at her work-smock, her jeans and sandalled feet.

'I can't go to the Schloss like this. I shall have to change,' she said.

His ironic smile acknowledged her surrender. 'No hurry,' he said easily. 'It's far from the first time I've waited on a lady claiming either she 'hasn't a thing to wear' or that she 'can't possibly go' in the clothes she has on. And I haven't invited the Baronin until one o'clock for half-past, so we have time on our hands meanwhile.'

Not to be outdone in this velvet-glove show of politeness, Juliet said, 'May I offer you a drink while you are waiting?' But he declined, saying they would drink in the bar with the Baronin before the meal.

Going into her room and closing the door, Juliet was thinking, You *bet* it isn't the first time for him! With those Nordic looks and that debonair assurance of his on the Innsgort road that he was the welcome answer to any travelling maiden's prayer—you bet he was no stranger to his girl-friends' ante-rooms while they prinked to be taken out by him to luncheon, dinner or whatever! Well, she wasn't prinking; she was just changing to have lunch with Magda von Boden as much as with him. But following that thought came another. For her, here, it *was* the first time of changing next door to a man who was waiting to take her out. Gerhard had always called for her at the Konstats' and though, since her return to the Lake, she had been out with friends from Gutbach or Munich, it had always been with married couples or a party.

So not the first time for him. But the first time for her. And hard upon that thought came a question—was he married?

If he were, it could mean she had made a two-deep enemy instead of a formidable enough one. But on reflection she felt pretty sure he was single. If he were married and had known real love, he couldn't have judged her so harshly for refusing to marry Gerhard without it.

She changed into a blue-and-white full swirling skirt and a white silk shirt and tied her hair into a pony-tail. Glad that convention didn't now require gloves and hat for a luncheon date, she swung a shoulder bag and went to join Karl Adler, prepared to set out with him for the Schloss.

But he said again, 'No hurry. Before we join the Baronin I'd appreciate it if you would tell me why, last night, you kept from me your intention to abandon the School and go back to England very shortly. When the hotel finally closes, in fact?'

How had he learned it? 'Probably,' Juliet said levelly, 'because I didn't consider it was any concern of yours.'

His nod appeared to agree. 'Though a very sudden switch of plan, wasn't it, your decision to see out the lease of this place, considering that the people I've

been seeing this morning were all surprised to hear
that you weren't leaving very soon?'

She had warned Magda not to tell him, but she
should have foreseen that he might hear it from any one
of her neighbours. At a disadvantage, 'It was a sudden
decision,' she admitted.

'Almost lightning, one might say? And at the sting
of a spur?'

'A spur?' she was losing command of this exchange.

'Uh-huh. The spur of my offer for your lease, which
you were determined not to cede to me. Up to that
point you had meant to throw in your hand and run
away—a second time?'

She turned indignant eyes upon him. 'I did *not* "run
away" the first time! When Gerhard finally accepted
that I wouldn't marry him, he made it virtually impossible for me to stay, and you've neither the right
nor enough knowledge to judge otherwise!'

'Very well, though I doubt if you would protest so
much if you hadn't suffered some conscience towards
him. Meanwhile, this time you were getting out because of the loss of the hotel's custom for your wares,
and there being no summer employment there any
longer for your workers. Right?'

'You *have* done your homework well!' She couldn't
resist the gibe. 'But yes, that's more or less how
matters stood—— As they stand,' she corrected herself.
'They haven't altered overnight.'

'Exactly,' he agreed crisply. 'It is only you who have
changed course?'

'You could put it like that.'

'And we know why.' He paused. 'Ever heard, have
you, Miss Harmon, of the ostrich's habit of burying
its head in the sand?'

'Of course.'

'And a very ill-advised procedure for humans, I've always thought. Consider the gritty effect on the eyes, the ears, the nostrils, the mouth——!'

'Thanks for the unnecessary warning. I've never tried it, and I'm not trying it now. I know precisely what I'm doing. And how. And why,' Juliet said.

The blue eyes widened almost disarmingly. 'But I've already told you—we both know why. It's to foil me—isn't it?' he urged.

She inclined her head. 'As long as you realise that it *was*, and may continue to be, if you persist in your claim on my tenancy.'

He acknowledged, 'I do realise it, and though I needed your confirmation of it, I haven't been long in doubt of your motive. If I may say so, hostility emanates from you like an aura.' He lunged upright from the window-ledge against which he had been leaning, and gestured her towards the door. 'But now you've been frank with facts which puzzled me, shall we go?'

She held back. 'Are you quite sure you still want to invite me to lunch with you?' she said.

'*In the circumstances*'—his short laugh and his echo mocked her—'I wouldn't miss it for the world! Come along——' His hand, firm beneath her elbow, amounted to a command. And intrigued against her will, aware that some nerve within her had responded electrically to his touch, Juliet went along.

The road which climbed to the Schloss was a succession of hairpin bends to the point where the castle itself stood out against the higher mounting backcloth of forest behind it. It was surrounded by a walled outer courtyard which served as a car park; a great archway, gated with wrought iron, led to an inner court and the main entrance doors. When she had adapted the building to the service of her guests, the Baronin had kept for her private use a self-contained octagonal tower attached to the east wing. Its height surmounted all but the massive central structure, and looking at it as he and Juliet crossed the courtyard, Karl Adler remarked, 'A real Rapunzel turret, that. You know the story, of course?'

She nodded yes.

'Makes one deplore, doesn't it, the invention of the domestic lift, when obviously the really ardent suitor would much prefer the romance of climbing up a rope of his lady's hair?'

'Would he? Though I'd think she might rather he made use of the lift.'

'So that he could reach her the faster? I doubt it, considering a woman's inveterate need, whether she is saying Yes to him or No, to make a man's approach to her as fraught as she can. For instance the hazard of that rope of hair. Or again——'

He paused for so long that at last Juliet was constrained to prompt, 'Or again——?'

'Well, such as when a stranger attempts an innocently friendly pass, the lady implies that his passport to her favour must be his production of his own lunch-packet. That does tend to turn a man off.'

She uttered a small gasp. 'I didn't say or imply anything of the sort!' she denied.

She might not have spoken. '——And of course, on again,' he said, as if in continuation of his own thought.

'And what do you mean by *that*—"on again"?'

He laughed. 'I assure you—in this instance, nothing

more menacing to the lady's virtue than our stranger
intended by his original plan for a chat in the sun with
an attractive fellow-traveller. No, all I meant by "on"
was that, their Fates ruling that they meet again, he
could find himself with an added zest for their second
round of hostilities. Wouldn't you think that possible?'

Of her own reaction, she thought, it was more than
possible. It had happened. She was relishing the situation. But denying him the satisfaction of hearing she
had given any thought to the matter, she said nothing
as they entered the wide hall, now furnished with a
reception desk and elevators for both guests and lug-
gage, flanking the magnificent main staircase.

The Baronin was awaiting them in the bar. She
greeted Juliet with a kiss on either cheek and Karl
Adler bent over her hand. There, and later at table,
their conversation was the small talk of cordial, if not
intimate friends; it went easily, considering the undercurrents running between herself and Karl Adler,
thought Juliet. No one would guess he had more or
less pressganged her into attending a business luncheon, since he did not attempt to touch upon any of
the issues between them.

It was towards the end of the meal that the Baronin
looked about her at the otherwise empty dining-room
and remarked with seeming irrelevance, 'Once, at Gib-
raltar, I joined a ship on its way back to Hamburg
from the Far East and found most of the amenities
and services already folded away—the swimming-pool
emptied, the library closed, even a great many items on
the excellent menus "off" for the last few hundred
miles of the voyage. And now——' she paused and
sighed, shaking her head.

'Now?' Karl Adler prompted gently.

'Well now, I am thinking, it is the same here. One or two guests remaining, but near the end of their stay; my staff depleted, my wine-cellars not what they were. It is the end of the Schloss as an hotel, as it was the tag-end of the voyage for that ship, and I feel I should apologise for such shortcomings as I know there are.'

Both Juliet and her host murmured sympathetic disclaimers, and there was silence until he questioned, 'Sad as it is for you, Baronin, must it be so? Is it inevitable—the closure of the hotel?'

'It's a decision I've had to come to,' she told him. 'I've carried the place on my shoulders, as it were, for ten years now. But I am old, and I want to retire—into my tower, perhaps to knit and dream my time away. Yes, it is inevitable, I'm afraid.'

'You are not to be persuaded that it needn't be? That the goodwill alone must be worth a very great deal?' he urged.

She drew herself up. 'I couldn't think of selling the goodwill into new ownership. Out of the question, that.'

Karl Adler said, 'I was thinking rather of management, Baronin.'

She smiled wryly. 'I have *tried* managers—at the end of a successful third year and again at the seventh. Both were disastrous experiments. No.'

'Even though I can recommend someone personally? A woman whose experience is of the very highest order. Cosmopolitan experience, at that—American, English. A friend whom I know to be free at the moment?'

Magda von Boden mused, 'A manager? A woman? A friend, you say?'

'Of long standing, yes. She was Munich-born, but

she has only recently come back to the city. Frau Ilse Krantz, her name.'

'Frau? She is married?'

'A divorcee from an unfortunate marriage. I knew her before she went into that.'

'Ah,' said the Baronin. And then, 'But it is quite impossible. It is too late. You talk of goodwill, but I have already lost all I had. I have taken no summer bookings, and the agencies have told their clients that to apply would be useless. And I have got rid of most of my staff.'

Karl Adler's gesture brushed aside such objections as trivial.

'You could advertise widely again—even make capital out of your decision to re-open. The hotel a triumphant phoenix, risen from its ashes—how about that? So—may I send Ilse Krantz to see you, Baronin?'

She appeared to hesitate. 'Perhaps. You must let me think about it, Herr Adler, please.'

'Of course.' He poured wine again for her and for Juliet, and his next remark was addressed to her.

'You ski, I think, Miss Harmon?'

As if he didn't know that, from their encounter on the Innsgort road! Not to be outdone in polite-sounding finesse, she asked, 'You too?'

'When I can make time, or am reasonably near some good slopes.' He turned to the Baronin. 'I was thinking of inviting Miss Harmon to join me in a day up at Innsgort, if she would.'

The Baronin beamed. 'An excellent idea! Julie loves to ski, and she is good. Julie, you must accept before it is too late, before the season closes.'

'I——' Juliet was thinking, not only of her skis, her

boots, her snow-goggles, probably already sold second-hand from the ski-master's shop, but with surprise that Magda, who must know just how she felt towards Karl Adler's demands, should suppose she would be willing to ski with him or that she had accepted his invitation to luncheon in any melting spirit.

But seeing that they were waiting for her to go on, she temporised with, 'I'm afraid that now I have decided to carry on with the School, I shan't have much free time for skiing.'

To which, for all the world as if she were a society mamma, anxious that her débutante daughter shouldn't miss a date with an eligible male, the Baronin said, 'Nonsense, dear. You've always made a little time for skiing until now. And if you delay, you stand the chance of missing the last of the good conditions.' And Karl Adler agreed with her.

'Exactly. I shall bring my gear the next time I come over,' ignoring Juliet as if she weren't there, or as if she were a child for whose caprice the grown-ups had to make allowances.

A few minutes later the Baronin rose, 'collecting' Juliet with her eye as, at countless elegant dinner-parties in her time, she had gathered her lady guests to retire to a drawing-room to await the gentlemen after their port and cigars.

On this occasion their host was not long in following them, saying he was at Juliet's disposal when she wanted to go home. In the car he remarked, 'The Baronin seems very fond of you.'

'As I am of her,' Juliet said.

'She would have liked you to marry Gerhard?'

'She has never criticised me for refusing him. She happens,' Juliet added pointedly, 'to be generous enough to allow people to make their own decisions about their lives, without blaming them or offering unasked advice.'

'I see. Admirably detached. All the same, mightn't she be glad for you to marry—period? Perhaps with a view to keeping you near her, here on the Lake or at least in Bavaria? After all, dowager ladies who've been happily married themselves often want to enlist their young protégées into the same league, don't they?'

Needing to deny her own small suspicion, Juliet snapped, 'The Baronin has never attempted any match-making for me, if that's what you mean.'

He agreed blandly, 'That's what I meant. But—never? Possibly knowing with rare wisdom that she might have first to disabuse you of some preconceived image of the German male as a husband?'

'Knowing, I hope and believe, that I would never marry any man who had been chosen *for* me—English, German, Tahitian or whoever!'

'Ah—the Engländer notably a poor lover; the German reputed to want only a yes-woman in the bed, the kitchen and the nursery; the Tahitian possibly with bizarre habits? Well, I can't plead the cause of either the first or the third, but I assure you that we Germans expect and mean to get more from our women than that they be submissive to our lovemaking, good plain cooks and dutiful mothers.' He tilted a glance. 'Would you care for me to enumerate—with details?'

She feigned indifference. 'Need you bother?'

'As a prejudice-dispelling exercise, yes. For instance —charm, spirit, self-dependence only to a certain point; enough visible allure to make her man the envy of every other male in sight; response, sur-render——'

'What's the difference between submission and surrender?'

'Plenty,' he parried. 'Submission is merely servile. Surrender needs to be worked for, earned.'

'And if it isn't forthcoming, I suppose the jackboot of command can always be brought into action?'

'Shouldn't be necessary. Given flair, expertise with your sex and a skilful playing of the field before making his choice, a man can usually get response from where he has wittingly chosen to look for it.'

'That's just blatant arrogance!' Juliet flared.

'On the contrary, a statement of cold fact—that nature having made him the chooser and the woman the chosen, he has the right to call the tune. Or to vary the metaphor—to hunt the quarry into the ground.' He paused, then laughed shortly. 'Let's see, where were we before we launched on this battle of the sexes?' Ah, I remember—you snubbed my suggestion that the Baronin might have marital plans for you. But you know she approves of your not leaving the Lake?'

'I think she will be glad when she understands the reasons for my staying.'

'Though can you be entirely truthful about them?'

Juliet caught her breath. 'Truthful? Of course. Why shouldn't I be?'

'Only that I wonder if it has occurred to you, the extent to which your stand in the matter of your lease could adversely affect the Baronin's affairs?'

She turned puzzled eyes his way. 'Harm her affairs? I don't understand?' she queried.

'Simple. Though we have taken over the project from Hartung, we haven't yet signed the deal for the von Boden timber and without freedom of action to build a sawmill, my directors might have second thoughts about concluding the deal. You see?'

She 'saw' the implied threat so well that her rejection of it was explosive. 'That—that's *blackmail*!' she flung at him. 'Using my feeling for the Baronin to force my hand! How dare you!'

His response, totally unexpected, was to reach to touch her knee with the patting motion he might use for the head of a dog or to soothe an angry child, and she jerked away from under it.

'Calm down, calm down!' he urged. 'I was merely putting all the facts—and the possibilities, remote as they are—before you. For instance, I don't envisage for a moment that we shan't do business for the timber, and you and your fellow tenants can only hold us up for a limited time. So—no blackmail intended. No need.'

'In other words, you only meant to put doubt in my mind as to whether I'm right in deciding to stay. You admit I can't really harm the Baronin and that I can't outwit you for good. But you are determined that I shall question my motives, and worry about them. *Very* clever, Herr Adler!' she raged. 'Diabolically so. But may I tell you one thing, and ask you one? The first—I am not worrying, and I'm not doubting, you can't frighten me into either with empty threats. And the other—since you have so low an opinion of me for more than one reason, why bother with me again after you had my firm No to your scheme? Why, for instance, invite me to a business luncheon at which the only business discussed had nothing to do with me? And why, even more ludicrously, go through the motions of pretending you'd like my company on a skiing trip? It couldn't have been just for something to say, for I should think you are rarely at a loss for—

for uninvited openings. So perhaps you will tell me why?'

They had reached the School and having stopped the car, he was free to turn to face her. It incensed her still further that there seemed to be a hint of amusement in the blue of his eyes, as he mused, mock-sagely, 'Mm —a fair question, that.'

'*I* think so.'

'Yes. And here's one for you. When you've got yourself an opponent who seems worthy of your steel and you've rehearsed all the arguments with which you mean to fell him, tell me—don't you ever feel cheated if chance robs you of the opportunity?'

It was so true of herself in relation to him that she forgot her resolve to keep from him that she ever thought about him in his absence, and almost shouted, 'Yes!'

'Well then——?' He paused, seeming to think it a reasonable question.

'Well then?' she echoed.

'Just that I believe in making my own opportunities,' he said. And then, opening the car door for her and ready to move off, '*Auf Wiedersehen, mein kleiner Hitzkopf, Auf Wiedersehen!* Or, as you'd say in English, wouldn't you?—Here's to the next time!'

He left his 'little spitfire' at a total loss for a retort.

CHAPTER THREE

WHEN Wilhelm came that evening to do the stocktaking he reported that during the morning and after Karl Adler had seen Juliet home, he had called to put his proposition to the remainder of the shore-tenants, and that Wilhelm himself had seen fit to pass on to those concerned Juliet's decision to stay and to keep the School going.

'The ones who didn't know you were staying and would make work for them here thought it wise to let the Herr have his way,' he announced in answer to Juliet's eager question.

'Oh—— And the others? The ones you did have time to tell about me?'

'They asked the Herr where they would live while they were working at the School if their houses were to be pulled down, and when he told them his workmen would build chalets for them elsewhere on the estate and have them ready to move into before they were asked to move, they said No to him. If the School was staying, they were staying where they were. *Ist das nicht gut?*' Wilhelm concluded, beaming.

'Good? I'll say it's good!' Juliet praised. 'If we stand together, they can't win, these tycoon types, and before our leases run out they will *have* to think again. Let everyone know, will you, Wilhelm, that we'll try to start work again next week, and I'll give them a pep talk about the new outlets I'll find for selling our stuff, now that we shan't be having the hotel guests as customers?'

She hadn't the right, she knew, to give Wilhelm any

hint of Karl Adler's proposals to the Baronin about re-opening the hotel. He must have meant them to be confidential, causing her to wonder why he had broached them in front of herself. As, on the level of his reasons for making them, the Baronin was questioning too, she told Juliet when inviting her to evening coffee a couple of days after he had returned to Munich.

Juliet drove up to the Schloss after an early supper. She went to the private door to the tower and took the miniature lift to the sitting-room on the top floor, where Magda was seated behind a tray of silver appointments, ready to dispense coffee and little cherry almond cakes.

'Herr Adler couldn't be concerned for me, for he knows that if I sell the timber I can afford to stay here privately,' she said. 'And though he said before he left that when he has to come over, as he must frequently, he'd find it convenient to stay at the hotel, I can't think he would be quite so persuasive about it for that reason alone. It could be that, as a businessman, he can't bear to see the goodwill lapse. But I'm inclined to think that he has the interests of his friend Frau Krantz mainly in view, and he wants this opportunity for her. What do you say, Julie? Was that the impression you got?'

Juliet thought back over the discussion. 'He did make rather a key figure of her,' she admitted. 'Did he tell you any more about her before he left?'

'A little. It seems she is young—under thirty—to have been so successful in everything but her marriage. She hasn't actually managed a hotel, but she has handled all the publicity and the interior decorating and equipment and staffing for new ones in America and in England. She is bi-lingual, of course, and Herr Adler was so enthusiastic that, as I say, I did wonder just how close they may have been, since she has been free and back in Germany. He isn't married, you know, though Gerhard once told me he had quite a reputation—— But Gerhard was prejudiced, and I mustn't gossip. Anyway, Herr Adler is bringing Frau Krantz over and I have said I will see her. Because it would be nice if the hotel hadn't to die after all. Don't you agree, dear?' the Baronin concluded wistfully.

Juliet did, and said so. Apart from all that its closing would mean to the School, the thought of the Schloss standing forlorn and unused after the seasonal business it had known had always depressed her since her friend had first told her that it was to have no future as a hotel. 'When is Herr Adler bringing Frau Krantz?' she asked.

'He didn't say definitely. But quite soon, I think, judging as I do, that for him ideas and actions are almost simultaneous. A *very* dynamic man, with sound reasons, in his own view, for anything he does. Which reminds me,' the Baronin went on, 'that, having accepted that you and the shore-tenants mean to stay on until your leases run out, he could possibly want the hotel to continue, so that the School shouldn't lose the guests' custom that it has always had. What do you think?'

Juliet's reply was a short rueful laugh. 'It's an ingenious idea, but totally not on,' she said. 'For one thing, I doubt if Karl Adler will "accept" any stand of ours as final until he has failed to outwit us. He said as much to me—that there were ways in which he could force our hand. He even instanced one of them.'

'Oh dear, what?' queried the Baronin, distressed.

'A suggestion that if we insisted on our rights and

prevented the building of his sawmill, that might jeopardise your sale of the timber to Adler Classics. Oh, it's all right'—Juliet reassured her friend's nervous movement of disbelief—'he admitted that it wouldn't happen that way, but implying that if the threat made me doubt my own motives, that was all right by him. Which brings me to the second thing—he doesn't like me personally well enough to make any generous gesture towards me at all. Or to the School, because of me. Of that I'm quite certain.'

'Not like you? Oh, my dear, you must be mistaken!'

'I'm not,' Juliet insisted. 'What's more, he chose to judge me for "failing" Gerhard, as he put it. That I could *not* take.'

'But he——! Not like you now? No, that *I* cannot take, dear,' the Baronin declared. 'For if not, why should he have asked you to ski with him, tell me that?'

'Probably just making conversation.'

The Baronin decided for her, 'No, he wasn't doing that, and you know it. He wanted a date with you. And why should he choose to spend a whole day in your company, if he feels about you as you claim, and—as I'm afraid you may have let him guess—*you* feel about *him*?'

But feeling she couldn't justify or explain Karl Adler's warped reasons for seeking her out—reasons which, she had told him on parting from him, she understood and shared, Juliet took refuge in a noncommittal, 'I couldn't say,' adding, 'Anyway, I couldn't accept if I wanted to. For now I have no skiing things.'

'Then you did sell them after all?' The Baronin sighed. 'How very final you meant your departure to be. But now—now I'm so glad that you are still to be here, perhaps to see our phoenix rise again, who knows? And as for your relations with Karl Adler——'

'Which you can't expect to change very much, I'm afraid——'

To which the Baronin retorted with crisp finality, 'Though I shall try to understand them on both sides —I *hope*.'

It was to take days rather than weeks for the first effects of the takeover to bring changes to the region.

Initially there were strange cars parked at different points of the von Boden estate; strange men pacing the forest rides, grouping for discussion, surveying and marking off areas of timber and prospecting sites for the fellers' huts. But this was all that happened by the time Juliet had re-opened the School and had been gratified by the eager return of all her workers to their benches.

Advertisements in a Munich trade paper and the Gutbach *Tageblatt* brought Wilhelm two new students in wood-carving, and though at the winter season's end Juliet had allowed the workshops' raw material to run down to almost nothing, there were the traditional ways of rectifying that—the selection and carting of suitable woods from the forests with the estate ranger's permission, and the only obstacle ahead was the sale of the winter's stockpile of articles before more were added to swell it.

But that, Juliet claimed to Wilhelm and the others, was her problem and she would beat it—or else! Armed with her list of prospects and a case of samples, she would take to the road as the School's traveller, and she was in the stockroom early one morning, deciding what to take from it, when there was a knock at the house door and her glance from the stockroom window showed Karl Adler's car standing outside.

So! What did *he* want this time? Surely not——?
Her thoughts had flown to Magda's insistence that he
had really meant his invitation to her to ski, and a
second peep at his car showed that his gear was indeed
on board.

Really! As she went to open to him it was with
mixed feelings of annoyance and a little prickle of excitement which she could not explain.

'Good morning.'

'Good morning.' He was so tall that he had to stoop
to enter. 'We had a date. For a day's skiing. You'll remember?' he asked of her silence and her raised eye-
brows as she stood aside for him.

'It wasn't a date,' she said. 'We made no arrange-
ments.'

'Then, if you like, one of my manufactured opportunities for battle of which I warned you.'

'If it was *that*——! Anyway, I'm working.'

'On a Saturday? Well, I'm not. I'm on a pleasant
errand of introducing Frau Ilse Krantz to the Baronin,
to their common advantage, I hope. May I use your
telephone?'

The question was so abrupt and matter of fact that
she waved him to the instrument as she would have
done any caller who needed to use it. With his finger
on the dial he looked over his shoulder to remark, 'I'm
ringing the Schloss to let the Baronin know we are
as good as on our way——'

Juliet darted forward. 'You can't do that! I——!'

But he had got his connection and was giving his
message to someone. He rang off and said, 'That's that,
then. You're committed.' With a hand on her back he
made to propel her to the door of what he knew to be

her bedroom. But she resisted and faced round.

'I have no skiing things any longer. I sold them to the ski-master's shop, the last time I was up at Innsgort, the day we——'

'The day I didn't make the grade because you prefer to picnic alone, and you had brought only food for one? Well, this time there's a lunch hamper for two in the car. And if it helps any generous conscience you may have, you can always tell yourself you are abetting me in spending a day in which I have nothing better to do with my time. So go and get kitted up. There's no problem about skiing gear. You can hire for the day. I'll give you ten minutes, and I'll wait for you in the car.'

Why did she obey him? To avoid an undignified contradiction of his message to the Schloss, she told herself. But her honesty knew there was more to it than that.

If she had sent him away there would be something lacking from her solitary day. Her hands and her surface mind would have been busy with her work. But there would have been undercurrents of regret for having missed the cut-and-thrust of contention at which, given the openings, she believed she could be as ready-tongued as he. Missed the staircase wit, as it was called —the retorts with which you might have confounded your enemy, if they hadn't occurred to you too late. Well, she wasn't going to be at the mercy of their nagging. If he provoked her—and he would!—they were coming out.

Besides, the snow scene called—diamond sparkle, blue shadows, sugar coating of snow upon roofs, infinite silence and contrasting burn of sun to bite of wind. Juliet pulled on a thick sweater, got into boots and an anorak and went out to the car.

Strangely and to her relief, easy conversation did not prove too difficult. They drew each other's attention to the scenery. Karl asked her how well she skied and how often during the season she had made the trip to the slopes. He didn't know Innsgort well himself, he said, but seemed to have visited most of the more famous resorts of the Alpine region.

During their silences and while he talked with his eyes on the road ahead, she covertly watched his hands on the wheel, admiring his effortless control of the car in the difficult terrain, and thinking how this might have been for them, *if* he hadn't been related to Gerhard Minden, or if anything about their involuntary connection had been other than it was.

They might have met and talked, have found a common interest in skiing. If Karl had invited her today she would have known he genuinely wanted her company, not because, as he had taunted, he had nothing better to do. And if she had accepted there would have been a tacit agreement between them that if they enjoyed the day's talk and action and togetherness, there could be other such occasions for them.

But there wouldn't be. There was no reward to indulging the fantasy that any thread of awareness of each other ran between them. For it didn't. Yet why should her gaze be fascinated by the sight of his hands, or her imagination want to toy with the thought of their touch upon her own in real friendship? Why, in his dry smile, did she wish she could glimpse a trace of warmth for her, or in his questions a genuine need to know her better? And why, in heaven's name, considering her avowed hostility to him, should she be harbouring any thought of him as a man she could be drawn to, if only——?

Within sight of the little village of Innsgort across the last valley, he drew the car off the road, saying, 'It's early for lunch, but we may as well get it over, so that we can go straight up to the slopes when we arrive.'

On his knees on the springy turf, he opened the hamper, spread a cloth and anchored it with stones. He handed Juliet cutlery and plates and glasses to set out, produced a jar of pâté, unwrapped napkins containing sausage and rolled wafers of ham and hard-boiled eggs and sliced rye bread, took crisp sauerkraut and butter from insulated containers, and leaving her to arrange these, opened a bottle of Riesling.

He raised his glass. '*Prosit*—Juliet,' he said, making almost an afterthought of her name.

'*Prosit*,' she toasted in return, but couldn't bring herself to the false familiarity of 'Karl'.

She found she was hungry enough to enjoy both the food and the wine, and she commented lightly on his expertise in picnic menus.

It proved dangerous ground. 'Hm. Calls for a modicum of experience,' he allowed. 'But unlike you, I believe in catering for at least two varying palates, and though some women need more persuasion than others, I don't often find myself left to eat alone.'

It was both a provocative assertion of his self-assurance and another tilt at her initial rebuff of him, and she was convinced he had deliberately evoked the embarrassed blush she couldn't control.

He parked the car at the Sport Hotel in the village and they went on foot to the ski-school and shop, where Juliet was kitted out with hired skis and boots and hand-poles. They took the cable-car to the medium slopes and sat outside the snack-restaurant to don their skis.

Juliet's were taken peremptorily from her and strapped and adjusted before Karl attended to his own. Watching him bent over both tasks, she was conscious again of a physical attraction which, if things were to be different between them, she wouldn't have wanted to resist.

Goggled and ready, they set out a few metres apart. But the paths they took soon diverged; presently Karl was a speeding figure, as much a stranger as all the other brightly clad human dots on the slopes and, speeding herself, she was thrilled as always by the essential 'aloneness' and self-reliance of the sport; to be one in competition with this delicious God-given element, warmed by sun and buffeted by wind, was achievement, she felt.

At the foot of the slopes Karl was waiting for her, circling to meet her near the drag-lift which would take them back up. When one was free they braced themselves against its T-bar, and he supported her with an arm about her waist, as closely linked as to a sweetheart, though she felt, with as little awareness of her body, necessarily pressed to his, as if he were toting an insensate parcel up the hill.

They went down the slopes several times, then he tried the marked-out slalom course while she rested. Rejoining her at the end of his run, he asked, 'Do you venture the high slopes at all? If so, should we make them our grand finale?'

Juliet nodded her agreement and went with him to the car which would take them to the top run. She usually kept to these slopes but had occasionally used the higher ones, and guessed that he wouldn't execute his 'grand finale' if she didn't go too.

Up there it was like being on top of the world. At that late hour of the afternoon they had been the only passengers in the car and had watched the whole scene dwindle almost to nothing before them—human figures to pinpoints, cars to matchbox size and the village to a huddle of dolls' houses grouped round the pencil spire of the church.

Out on the *piste* with the long steep run before them, Juliet was seized with sudden panic. Supposing she couldn't do it? Made a fool of herself by falling, which for nuisance value had more threat to her pride than the dramatic risk of a broken limb? There was a prickle of apprehension at the base of her spine—no mood in which to set out, she knew, but in a spirit of bravado she went, croaking 'Ready!' to Karl before he called it to her.

He let her go first and did not overtake and pass her until she was smoothly running, her fears forgotten. This was the life! She found she was humming *Edelweiss*.

After a few hundred metres there was a slight upward gradient which broke her speed; then she was spinning down again ... then up, changing direction slightly ... then down, down, down, now and again seeing Karl ahead of her. He had suggested that as it was their last run, they should ski right down to the village, instead of taking the cable-car down from the medium slopes, and it was with a sense of heady achievement that she took the last steep drop above the activity about the car-stand. She was going to bypass it, and after that it would all be easy ...

Karl must have paused and waited for her at some

point on the run, for now, at some distance away, he
was level with her, and it was as he drew ahead again
that things began to go wrong for her.

Watching him, she hadn't been concentrating. She
had straightened her knees, made a mis-thrust with
her poles and her skis were sliding ominously apart,
out of control at the speed she was making. There were
levels ahead, but she wasn't going to reach them with
dignity or any kind of skill. She was going to crash, do
an ignominious somersault if no worse—and then, suddenly she wasn't, as Karl, speeding at an angle into her
path, was there to take her full weight against the hard
unyielding mass of his body. Less skilled than he was,
he could have brought them both down in a dangerous
flailing of skis and limbs. But as it was, they both kept
their feet as he steadied her with both arms so closely
round her that as she pulled off her goggles to look up
at him she could hardly bring his face into focus.

What she saw in the blue eyes was neither sympathy
nor the derision she deserved, but anger. He almost
shook her as he released her. 'Why, in pity's name,
couldn't you admit you had never done the high run
before?' he demanded. 'By the way you tackled that
last slope, you might never have left the nursery!'

'I *didn't* lie! I have come down from the top before,'
she blazed back at him. 'I managed the rest all right. It
was just that I lost concentration for a moment, and—
well, it could happen to anyone any time,' she finished
lamely.

His grim nod agreed. 'As you say, any time—but
could be once too often for the "anyone" of a tyro on a
gradient like that.'

Almost choking with chagrin, 'I am *not* a tyro!' she
denied.

'Well, you were acting like one when I came up with you—near to panic and without a clue.'

'And if you hadn't come up with me, I'd have taken a toss that would have been my own fault—and so what?'

'Perhaps,' he said carefully, 'it would be better if we didn't go too closely into "what". And no'—as she pulled down her raised goggles—'if you don't mind, we'll get out of our gear here and go down to the village by the car. Unless of course you are bent on doing an exhibition run, though I'd rather you didn't, on the whole.'

Juliet was tempted to defy him and refuse to go down by the car. But that meant discussing a meeting-time at the hotel, and for the moment she found parley with him about anything quite impossible.

They were separated in the cable-car which was full. Juliet returned her hired things to the shop. At the snack-bar above, Karl had suggested soup, and at the hotel, tea. But she had refused both, and it was not until they had taken to the road again in almost complete silence that she began to see her dudgeon as slightly ridiculous.

She had reacted to his scathing criticism as if she really cared about his opinion of her. But how could it matter that, on this one day which wouldn't be repeated, he had dubbed her roundly as foolhardy and a rotten skier? It didn't, of course. They had a great deal weightier issues at stake between them in the tomorrows ahead. Added to which, the nag of knowing that he had saved her from a disaster which she might not have been able to dismiss with an airy 'So what?' and the prospect of their having to share two hours more of icy withdrawal brought her first to a casual comment on the scenery, and then to the admission,

'You were right. I was being careless, and I *was* beginning to panic at the prospect of crashing.' But if she expected him to acknowledge her amend with grace, she was disappointed.

He said, 'Just as well to admit it. Six weeks or so of a limb in plaster for the sake of showing off can hardly be anyone's idea of hilarious fun.'

'I was not showing off!'

'Would you rather I suspected you were playing for a dramatic rescue by some knight-errant of the ice?'

'Don't be absurd. There was no one near me!'

'*I* was near you,' he observed mildly. 'Used you to ski with Gerhard?'

'At first. Later he wasn't fit enough.'

'You would have come up here to Innsgort for the day?'

'It's too far for a small car, there and back, in a day. We usually stayed overnight, at the weekend.'

'Where?'

'At the hotel.'

'Chastely in separate rooms, one trusts?'

The irony in his tone enraged her. Indignantly she matched it with, 'No! We always booked the honeymoon suite and laid on an orgy until dawn!'

For a split second his silence allowed her to think he believed her. Then he commented, 'That's a pretty acid sense of humour you have, Juliet Harmon. Doesn't it ever land you in trouble with your friends?'

'Only,' she raged, 'when trouble has been made *for* me. Traps laid, doubt of my word, biting sarcasm! You know perfectly well, for I've told you, that Gerhard and I were never lovers; that there was nothing of

—of that sort between us; that I had no idea he cared for me until——'

'Until you couldn't shut your eyes any longer to his need of you? You worked with him, played, drove, talked—but you didn't *want* to know, did you? Or if it's true that you didn't, what kind of ice are you made of? Do you ask me to believe that a girl can't sense a man's feelings about her, long before he spells them out?'

'Of some men she can know them. Of others, not.'

'Gerhard, you claim, being one of the "others"?'

'Yes. He was reserved, withdrawn . . . close.'

'And the "some men" who are so many open books —how many have you known?'

'One or two.'

'Interesting. And into which category would you put me, for example? Does the pricking of your intuitive thumbs tell you all that I think about you?'

Looking fixedly ahead, 'I hardly need to use my intuition on that, do I?' Juliet queried. 'You've made your opinion of me very clear.'

He greeted that with a short laugh. 'As if I couldn't guess you would count me among your transparent "one or two"! Predictable, overbearing, tasteless——'

'Not always predictable.'

'Come, that's something!' he mocked.

'But always consistent in your measurement of me as someone you feel you should despise—and do, most of the time.'

'And when I'm not actively expressing my contempt—what then?'

She turned her head slowly. 'That's where I don't understand you. Why, having judged me for what you think I am, you don't leave me severely alone. Today, for instance—this masquerade of our being friends. It was ridiculously artificial, and we're as much at odds now as we were before. So why?'

'You appeared to accept the reason I gave you—that it seemed a good way of spending an empty day.'

'*Mine* needn't have been empty.'

'But you came along.'

'You gave me no chance to refuse before you were ringing the Schloss to tell Magda it was settled that we were going.'

'Big Bad Wolf carrying off reluctant Maiden? You know perfectly well you'd have regretted refusing, if you had.'

'I should *not*!' But remembering her moment of truth while she had been changing, she felt her colour rise as she made the denial and knew that his swift glance along his shoulder had noted it.

He said calmly, 'You lie about as ineptly as you attempt feeble jokes. You know you'd have hated missing the chance to wither me with argument. A whole day in my company from which you'd let me emerge unscathed by your tongue? Perish the thought!'

Juliet gave up. Her dignity demanded it. 'If you've decided that this is why I came, then there's nothing more to be said,' she stated.

'And if that wasn't your reason for coming, what was? I'll do my best to believe you—if I can.'

But she scorned to answer that, and left him to conclude what he would from her silence which, as the powerful car ate up the miles, was only broken by either of them later with a cursory remark or two on the state of the road or the distance yet to be covered.

When they reached the School he helped her out

and handed her the anorak she had discarded in the warmth of the car.

'We shall be meeting later,' he said. 'The Baronin is expecting you to dinner.'

'She hadn't invited me. How do you know?'

'She asked me to invite you, to meet Ilse Krantz before we drive back to Munich tonight. Eight o'clock. I'll come down for you at a quarter to.'

'Please don't,' she urged quickly. 'I'll drive up myself.'

He didn't insist. 'As you please.' He turned as he was about to get into the car. 'Whether or not you achieved your object in joining me today, at least I outdid you in the matter of picnic courtesy, wouldn't you say?' he invited.

Belatedly she remembered that she hadn't thanked him. 'But of course,' she grudged. 'I've enjoyed the day.'

He sketched an ironic bow. 'Thank you. As for what the day did for me——'

So it was flippancy now in place of armed combat, was it? Matching the raillery in his tone, 'Yes, do tell me, what *did* it do for you?' she broke in, feigning a bright, spurious interest.

He shrugged. 'Offered me a breathing-space. An opportunity, as the French put it, *reculer pour mieux sauter*. Which means——'

'Thank you, I know what it means. Literally, to hold back in order to make a better jump,' she translated coldly.

'Exactly. A confidential spying on the enemy in readiness for the battle ahead. To which I'm sure you are spoiling to warn me, "Watch your step, Herr Adler, watch your step!"'

'How right you could be, at that,' she agreed. 'As far as I'm concerned, you should.'

'And believe me, Miss Harmon, I shall!' The audacious, goading confirmation of their continuing feud had the sting of a gadfly for her as she watched him drive away.

CHAPTER FOUR

AFTER that dinner-party Juliet was left in no doubt that in Karl Adler plus Ilse Krantz she had indeed acquired a two-deep enemy. For it was obvious that the other woman had heard all that he knew of her himself, with the consequence that her hostility to Juliet was barely veiled.

She was tall, with a matt-cream skin, tawny eyes and a wealth of russet hair which she wore in a heavy swathe at the nape of her neck. She was dressed in a trouser suit of thick white silk, and contrived to make Juliet feel overdressed in her floor-length, long-sleeved gown of brown velvet, with the laughing apology, 'You must think me terrible for not dressing. But I've been here all day, working with the Baronin, and I didn't know I'd be meeting guests for dinner.'

The Baronin, overhearing, put in, 'Just one guest only, Frau Krantz—Julie, who is a dear young friend. No one else.' To which Ilse Krantz murmured, 'Of course—*Julie*. You've told me how fond you are of her!' And then, head tilted, coaxing slightly, 'But mayn't I hope to be "Ilse" from now on, Baronin?'

Magda von Boden's paper-delicate cheeks flushed.

'But of course, if you wish it,' she said with well-bred politeness, though Juliet felt that she found the suggestion a little premature.

With the help of her own maid, the Baronin had prepared dinner herself in her tower apartment. As always, she was the ideal hostess, guiding the talk rather than dominating it, contributing little herself, drawing her guests out.

Ilse Krantz, clearly on no mere one-day Christian name terms with Karl Adler, was eager to claim to him the success of her survey of the hotel's possibilities under her management. She proposed to do this; she had advised the Baronin of the wisdom of that; Karl must get busy, laying on the new publicity; as soon as she could arrange her own affairs, she would be coming back to take up her quarters in the Schloss, and there seemed no reason why the first of the summer clients shouldn't be accommodated by the end of the month.

She threw Juliet a patronising smile. 'You see how busy we've had to be, while you've been keeping Karl out of mischief on the ski-slopes! Planning staffing, re-decorating, catering—the lot. Fun for some, while we others work!' And the Baronin interposed mildly,

'Of course it all needs more discussion. But as Frau'—she checked at the playful frown the younger woman sent her—'as Ilse says, we have achieved a certain agreement.' She added to Ilse, 'Do you plan to give up your Munich apartment when you move in here?'

Ilse shook her head. 'Oh, I think not. I have so many friends, and I entertain so much. I shall have to spend some of my time there still. Say at least my "half-days off". Besides, Karl tends to regard my place as his home-from-home, dropping in whenever he is free, or needs feminine company or relaxation, or both. Come now, Karl, admit that it's so?' she challenged him.

'As much as you are equally welcome at my place,' he said urbanely.

'Though, being a woman, I have to wait to be asked *there*!' she flashed. She turned to Juliet. 'Too bad, isn't it, that we can't stake a claim to our fancy, as the men can? Or perhaps you've found that it sometimes pays off to be a little more come-hither and willing than convention advises? I mean—though you English-women are supposed to be so cold and correct, isn't it possible that you are just as predatory under your skin as any Latin or Celt—or German for that matter?'

It was a deliberate taunt, but before Juliet could frame a retort, Karl Adler was chiding, 'Ilse, *mein Liebling*, aren't you assuming too much on too short an acquaintance? Now I, on a very slightly longer one with Miss Harmon, can assure you she is correct to a degree!'

Ilse pulled a face at him. 'She must be, if she has kept you at the arm's length of "Miss Harmon" until now. Do you really mean that you've been addressing each other as "Herr Adler" and "Miss Harmon" all day, even at *après-ski*?'

Not looking at her, but straight at Juliet with a glint of mischief in his eyes, he said, 'At Miss Harmon's wish, we didn't indulge in any *après-ski*. We came straight back.'

Ilse nodded mock-sagely at Juliet. '*Very* prudent of you to realise how little this character is to be trusted. An hour of *après-ski* in a bar, and——!' With a shrug and an oblique smile she left the rest to the imagina-tion, as the Baronin asked Karl if he didn't think Juliet a good skier.

When he didn't answer for a moment Juliet held her breath. Was he going to shame her in front of this supercilious girl-friend of his? But, again his glance as much on her as on his questioner, he said carefully, 'I'd say she has a flair amounting almost to extravagance,' which, though he couldn't have intended it as praise, had enough double-meaning to cause the Baronin to beam her approval.

'I knew you would find her an exciting partner,' she said, while Juliet, meeting his continued fixed gaze, wondered what quirk of gallantry had kept him from betraying her inept antics on that last slope.

He could have made a good story of it; have implied to the Baronin, 'A good skier? You must be joking!' But he had let her off. Why? Momentarily she allowed her own glance to signal thanks to him, and was rewarded with the faintest of conspiratorial smiles. However trivially, for the first time in their stormy relationship they were on the same side.

He and Ilse left for Munich soon after they had taken coffee. The Baronin detained Juliet for a while. She wasn't as sanguine for the hotel's future as Juliet had hoped to find her, and as Ilse had claimed they both were. But being incapable of judging anyone or anything without cause, for all her misgivings she seemed prepared to go ahead.

'I only fear,' she ventured, 'lest Frau Krantz should be trying for too much modernism. She criticises our furnishings as old-fashioned; says people expect up-to-date fitments in their rooms, such as built-in cupboards, rather than our antique *Kleiderschränke*—so roomy and, like all the rest of our furniture, so much in character with the age of the Schloss, I've always thought.'

'And so it is,' Juliet claimed. 'Every piece you have

is in keeping. Didn't you tell her that people who choose a German castle for a holiday don't expect to find it decked out New York penthouse style? They *want* huge oak wardrobes, fourposters—the lot!'

The Baronin smiled wryly. 'I wasn't *quite* so direct as that,' she admitted.

'But Magda, you should have been!'

'Not at this stage, dear. After all, Frau Krantz plans to attract some guests quite soon. But as most of these new-broom changes will take time, I can afford to wait a little to let matters develop before I give in. As you say, Frau Krantz'—Magda's pretty nose wrinkled—'oh dear, I'm to call her Ilse, aren't I? Well, though she may be wrong, I must try to be fair about this and give her her chance, don't you think?'

'I suppose so. Though you could be too fair,' counselled Juliet.

'But I must still try. Just as I told you I would try to appreciate your differences with Karl Adler,' her friend reminded her. And then mused, 'You know, I'm not at all sure that our new friend entirely approved of Karl Adler's invitation to you to go skiing with him. In fact, if I hadn't told her during the day how matters stood between you and him, I'd have said that some of her slightly waspish remarks showed that she was jealous of you. What do you think?'

Juliet laughed shortly. 'If you really made her understand about Karl Adler and me, jealous is the very last thing she could possibly be, and she must know it.'

The Baronin stuck to her point. 'All the same, he had kept to his word to invite you. And you did accept and go with him.'

'And in consequence I'm a little suspect for going?'

'Well——' the Baronin temporised.

'Even though his reason for asking me—he admitted it—was that it would give us the chance to go on working at our quarrel? Which, however hard it is to believe, happens to be true,' Juliet challenged.

'Dear me. And I'm to take it that you accepted for the same peculiar reason?'

'More or less,' Juliet admitted. 'Anyway, certainly from no motives that could make Ilse Krantz jealous. Simply, I think, to—well, to keep my end up; not to be the first to cry Pax.'

'How very odd, dear. And surely the most bizarre reason ever for two young people's willingness to spend several hours of an open-air day together! But tell me —how, in these strange circumstances—over a picnic lunch and a jolly time on the slopes—did your quarrel progress?'

Juliet accused, 'You haven't believed a word I've told you. And of course you are right about the quarrel, just for today. We didn't pursue it actively, but that doesn't mean it has gone away, or lessened or changed. Because really, Magda, Karl Adler and I are not "two young people" in the sense you mean. He can't forgive me for what he sees as my desertion of Gerhard when he needed me, and I can't forgive him for not understanding that I was right to refuse to marry Gerhard without loving him. And on top of all that, there's his tyrannic demand for my land, and my determination that he shan't have it. So if you or Ilse Krantz or anyone can see the makings of an affair for us in that setup, then you are sadly misguided optimists, I'd say.'

The Baronin nodded. 'I see. You make it very clear that I was mistaken and Ilse Krantz has no reason to fear her own possession of Karl Adler's interest is threatened by you.'

'You think she has his interest?'

'Rightly or wrongly, I think she assumes she has—don't you?' said the Baronin.

Juliet wished she hadn't asked the question.

It seemed incredible that in the course of the next few weeks the face of the lake region could change so much. Where at first there had been the few strangers and their few cars, now there were hordes of men and musters of lorries and tractors, chugging along the forest rides and parked in the clearings. Here and there the slopes already began to look denuded of their trees, and great chain-bound loads of timber were ferried out daily.

With their housing as yet unbuilt, the timbermen commuted over from Gutbach and further afield, and as never before Rutgen village prospered on their custom for food and beer and their own and their vehicles' emergency needs. An early consequence of the influx was that, though Frau Konstat remained loyal to the School's catering rota, she was often the only helper to turn up to serve Juliet's workers and students with their midday snacks. There was too good money to be earned at part-time work in the village *Wirtshaus* for people to make themselves cheap by working for nothing at the School. It was understandable, but it made difficulties, and there were many noons when Juliet herself donned an apron and dispensed goulash and sausage and canned beer at the snack-bar.

It was disturbing when a couple of her skilled workers gave her notice and joined the ranks of the timbermen for better pay. Wilhelm Konstat grumbled, 'It is the thin end of the wedge; in time the Herr will have all of us working for him, not for ourselves.' But this Juliet vehemently denied. They were doing well, weren't they? Soon they would be selling again to the hotel, and her own salesmanship should bring in as many orders as they could handle. And at least their tenancies were safe. 'The Herr' could do nothing about *them*, could he?

At that stage she admitted to no one that there were hazards she should perhaps have foreseen and had not. She was finding that too many of her selling trips brought too few results, for the simple reason that to both the retailers and the wholesalers she visited she was offering her wares too late.

The tourist season was already upon them. Did she not realise that they had stocked up with souvenirs months ago? they asked, sometimes pityingly, sometimes rudely. Yes, of course they would file the Fräulein's card, and next buying season perhaps— At the end of each of the two days a week she gave to selling, Juliet's smile became more fixed and mechanical in direct ratio to the hours she spent waiting to be seen by the buyers and the number of the stairs she had climbed to their offices.

It was when she was leaving the trade entrance of a department store on the Röder Strasse in Munich one lunchtime that she came face to face with Karl Adler. He offered his hand. 'Well, well!' he said in place of a formal greeting. There was a car park across the street, and he was going to collect his car. Could he drop her anywhere? he wanted to know.

She hesitated, tempted to accept. She had breakfasted soon after dawn, her feet ached and the nearest restaurant she could afford was several streets away. Perhaps accepting a lift there wasn't too abject a surrender to the enemy. 'Thank you,' she said distantly. 'You are kind.'

In his car, 'Where to?' he asked.

'I was going to lunch at the Goldener Bückling on Schwan Platz. Do you know it? It's——'

He nodded. 'I know it. But a bit of a dump, surely? We can do better than that, I think.'

'*I* can't do better than that,' she said sharply.

'But *we* can. I'm hungry, and I'm lunching too. Die Silberkanne, I think. Come along.'

'I haven't said yet that I am lunching with you,' Juliet pointed out—too rudely, she knew.

'If you are letting me drive you to Die Silberkanne, you are,' he retorted with finality. 'I'm known there, and to part with an attractive guest at the door would be considered highly eccentric. Bad for my reputation.'

'As a frequent escort of—allegedly—attractive guests?'

'Naturally. I pride myself on a certain taste in such matters, and as I've told you, I prefer to eat socially, rather than alone,' he said blandly, confirming for Juliet a picture of all the women he must have escorted to the city's top restaurants, which she did not relish very much.

He must have heard from either Ilse or the Baronin of her sales drive, for when they had been seated by the head waiter and he had consulted her on the menu, he asked her how she was doing.

'For a beginning, pretty well,' she hedged.

'You aren't finding you are offering your goods to the buyers too late for this season?'

What right had he to be so shrewd? 'Perhaps for one or two,' she admitted, adding a desperate, 'But they are all showing interest, long-term.'

'Have you tried Grünwehr? Kleinmayer?' he asked, naming two department stores.

'They are on my list. I was going to Kleinmayer this afternoon.'

'We do business with them both. I'll drive you to Kleinmayer when we leave here.'

'Thank you.'

Towards the end of the meal, a little mellowed by the good food and his choice of wine, she ventured,

'I feel I ought to thank you for keeping from the Baronin and Frau Krantz your real opinion of my skiing when the Baronin asked you about it.'

He laughed shortly. 'I was truthful. I told them you had flair—which you have. To the point of an extravagance which might well have put us both in hospital with a limb or two in traction—also true.'

'You didn't add that last bit.'

'I left it to their imagination.'

'But Magda, at least, thought you were praising me!'

'Was it my fault if her fond imagination led her that way? Besides, as your accepted escort that day, I couldn't let you lose face over a triviality like that.'

'You mean—considering all the face you think you can make me lose in the future?' she flared involuntarily.

'Come, come now!' His tone held derisive reproof. 'What general ever revealed to the enemy his campaign strategy?'

'For that is all your seeking of my company can possibly amount to—mere strategy, tactics?' she riposted.

'I told you why I invited you to Innsgort.'

'Yes, I know—because you saw a boring day ahead,

and the French bit about second jumps. But today?'

'We met by accident today,' he reminded her.

'When you could have acknowledged me and walked on. Instead you make it difficult for me to refuse to lunch with you at a place like this and—and seem to show interest, which can't be genuine, considering all you know of me and think of me, and none of it favourable. So *why*?'

Determinedly she held his glance, daring him to evade so direct an attack. But he did. Unmoved, evenly, he countered, 'Seems to me you've answered your own question—that it's tactics on my part. What else?' Then he looked at his watch and rose. 'Will you excuse me? I have to telephone. Then we'll be on our way.'

He left her to a strange sense of defeat. Of emptiness. Of an awareness that between the beginning of her tirade and its end, something cruelly revealing had happened. By the time she had uttered that last 'Why?' she hadn't meant it as an attack, but an appeal ... a cry that hadn't been answered.

She had wanted him to tell her she was wrong; that, both times, his purpose had been his male need to know more of her as a woman; at least that he had sought her company because it had some sort of value for him. But nothing had come, and without it she felt bereft; as rejected as by a lover's brutal telling that he had finished with her ...

A lover? Thinking of love in the same breath as of Karl Adler? How could she? She must be mad! She couldn't have fallen in love with a man with whom she was so much at odds, as he was equally with her. It wasn't possible. In love there had to be a mutual reaching-out, a tenderness, a need to explore with

every shared, pleasured sense—none of which she had
experienced at this man's hands. Between them there
was only a wary circling of the issues, a kind of ready-
ing of weapons for future use. Or so he hinted it was
for him. But for her—what? If she didn't, couldn't,
didn't want to tear clear of this madness—what then?

When he rejoined her she looked at him with shy
new eyes, still seeking, if not hoping for, a rewarding
change in touch or voice or look of which she could
make something she could treasure. But of course
there was nothing different about him. He was the self-
assured stranger of the Innsgort road and now her
enemy; ready to parley with her for his own ends, but
with reason, in his own estimation, to regard her with
scorn.

He drove her to the Kleinmayer trade entrance and
told her that a Herr Bezold was the buyer she must see.
She thanked him for the lift and went up the stairs to
an outer office where two other travellers were waiting when she handed her card to a girl clerk. Having
by now learned the art of patience, she sat down, prepared to take her turn after them.

But in a very few minutes the girl answered a buzzer
and beckoned to her. 'Herr Bezold will see you now,
Fräulein Harmon.'

Juliet rose, but hesitated, glancing at the two men.
'It's not my——' she began.

'Herr Bezold is waiting, Fräulein,' said the girl,
sounding bored, and though Juliet felt guilty of breach-
ing an accepted trade code, she had no choice but to
obey.

Herr Bezold was a man of few words and swift decisions. Twenty minutes later he had completed plac-
ing a substantial order with her, and she was repack-

ing her samples when the girl clerk opened the door
to announce to her chief, 'Herr Adler to see you, sir,'
and Karl followed her in.

He and Herr Bezold greeted each other and shook
hands. 'A word or two about that dining-suite consignment. But one moment first,' Karl told the other
man, and turned to Juliet.

'Have you finished for the day?' he asked.

'I think so, yes.'

'You came over by car? Where is it parked?'

She told him, and he said, 'If you'll wait for me in
the lobby, I'll drive you there. It's on my way.'

He came out to her presently and took her sample
case from her. 'How did it go?' he asked.

'Very well indeed. It was my best order of the day.'

'But not the only one?'

'Oh no.' (After all, a quarter-dozen ashtrays and a
cigar-box which were her only other meagre pickings
did count as an order, didn't they?)

Arrived at her garage she thanked him for the lift
and left the car, only to be puzzled by the empty
office and the iron grid gates which barred the forecourt of the place. She faced about, seeing that Karl
had not yet driven off.

'It's closed,' she announced blankly.

'At this hour? It can't be.' He got out and joined
her, pointed to a notice pinned to the gates. 'It can,'
he contradicted himself. 'Didn't you read this?'

She read it then. 'They should have warned me!'
she protested.

'They probably thought you could read—that,
owing to tomorrow's public holiday, all cars parked on
today's ticket should be collected by two o'clock.
They've taken the rest of the day off.'

'They should have told me as well, for I could have fetched mine earlier.' She bit her lip in vexation. 'Now what do I do?' asking it of herself, thinking aloud. 'Train, I suppose, to Gutbach and a taxi from there.'

'The alternative being that I drive you.'

She shook her head. 'Oh no. That's out of the question.'

'Even though I was going out later to the Schloss for dinner with Ilse and the Baronin?'

She looked at him doubtfully. 'You really were?'

'And spending the night and tomorrow's feast-day. I have to go back to my office and my apartment first. But after that we can be on our way. Get in.'

On the huge forecourt of Adler Classics he left her in the car and was gone for half an hour. At the block where he had his apartment, facing the English Gardens, he suggested she go up to it with him.

'If you stay here, you may be badgered by the police to move the car on,' he advised when she hesitated.

The living-room of his apartment on the mezzanine floor was carpeted with blue rugs on parquet and furnished with low claw-legged tables, cushioned wooden chairs and free-standing book-fitments. The wall decorations were tapestried; there were antique bowls and jars of coloured porcelain on the tables, and a single framed photograph on the open flap of a writing-desk.

It was signed *'Für Karl'* with a date Juliet could not read and was unmistakably of Ilse Krantz, bare-shouldered and swan-necked; a studio pose, seductive to a degree.

Was that why Karl had urged her to come up to the apartment? Juliet wondered. So that her sight of the photograph should spell out to her his intimacy with

Ilse? But she dismissed the idea. As if he cared about her opinion of his relationship with Ilse! He couldn't guess at her heightened awareness of his attraction for her and be warning her off ... could he? The very possibility chilled her.

He did not keep her long while he changed from city clothes to slacks and an open-necked shirt, the thin silk of which, clinging to his diaphragm, emphasised the muscularity which rippled beneath the golden bronze of his skin. The wide spread of the shirt's collar revealed the twin hollows at the base of his throat and, resist the urge as she would, Juliet found herself wanting to trace a fingertip touch from there along the line of his collarbone. The skin would be satin-smooth, warm ... and the folly of indulging the wish quite, quite mad!

Before they left the city he bought extravagant sheaves of flowers for the Baronin and Ilse, and dropped a small posy of violets into Juliet's lap with the comment, 'A modest tribute to a semi-reluctant guest.'

'Thank you.' Scorning to protest with a conventional 'You really shouldn't——' she smelled the sweetness of the posy, then clasped it in her hands, idle on her lap. They were travelling by the Autobahn; the car's speed was constant, the roadside view dull. She had been up at dawn and this easeful uniformity acted as a lullaby. Conscious that she was drowsing, she scolded herself and managed to jerk awake more than once. But it was happening again and she couldn't help it. Her eyelids were drooping deliciously, the peace was exquisite. Just a few minutes—she would allow herself no more ... and after that was aware of nothing for an unknown period that was lost to her for ever.

She half-woke—to the cupping of her face between cool hands and the pressure of lips upon hers in a long kiss to which her mouth was drowsily yielding ... responding in desire.

Who——? How——? She stirred, touched the wrists of the hands about her chin, felt bare arms above the wrists, and came to with a gasp. The car was standing at her own door; she saw the outline of the house gables against the twilight sky—over the shoulder of Karl who was looming above her, his head lifted now, watching her.

For the space of a pounding heartbeat she stared back at him. 'You kissed me,' she accused.

'Yes,' he nodded.

'But why should you—need to?'

'Isn't it the classic method of waking a lady?'

'I was only dozing!'

'Dozing? You haven't been among those present for the last thirty kilometres! You were so far under that it was a choice between assault and battery, bawling in your ear or the pleasurable method I used.'

'*Pleasurable?*' she echoed. 'To kiss *me?*'

'Why not? Asleep, you were attractively vulnerable, and it could be said I was only obeying the same healthy male instinct which made me invite myself to lunch with you on the Innsgort road. A pretty girl— the opportunity of finding her alone—or asleep—why, it would be flying in the face of Nature for a man to pass up such a chance!'

She recognised ridicule and it stung. 'Just any pretty girl, hm? Or even, perhaps, any *girl*?' she taunted.

'When one is in the mood, perhaps. Though naturally there's more piquancy to choosing to kiss a pretty one.'

'As if I'd have let you kiss me that day, just because we happened to be there! And you wouldn't have dared to try!'

'Oh, I don't know. Who can tell how we might have fraternised if I'd been allowed to share your sausage platter and whatever wine you had brought along?'

'I certainly shouldn't have let you kiss me then, and since, it's obvious you couldn't want to. Which makes —all this quite pointless——'

While she had slept she had relaxed in her seat and now she pushed herself upright—a movement which brought her so close to Karl that it should have caused his recoil. But it did not. His thumb flicked open the buckle of her seat-belt and he caught her to him, arching her body into the unyielding curve of his own.

So near now that his breath fanned her face, he murmured, 'Pointless, as you say—this fuss about a kiss claimed on the spur of the moment!' and with studied deliberation took her mouth again.

She twisted away, but he did not let her go. Almost amusedly he said, 'There are kisses and kisses—didn't you know? Some with the emotional impact of an earthquake, others exchanged against one's better judgment, others again——'

She bore down on his encircling arms with both hands and he released her, straightening and facing forward. 'You can spare me the list of all the kinds you've sampled at—at other people's expense!' she panted. 'So now will you please let me get out, and— and I'm sorry I had to trouble you to drive me home!'

'Don't mention it. It was a privilege,' he said, and

as he opened the car door for her he indicated the violets.

'Are you sure you aren't fighting an urge to throw them in my face?' he mocked her mortification.

Juliet looked down at them, then back at him, shaking her head. 'Nothing about this silly argument is their fault. I wouldn't demean them so,' she said.

He gave no sign that the barb had gone home. She didn't look back again, but knew he waited until she had reached and opened her door before he drove away. Then she watched the car out of sight.

She was trembling, not too far from tears. Of anger? Shame? Or of regret? All of them in a tangle of emotion she couldn't analyse. Karl had kissed her, admitting to a passing impulse which had meant nothing to him. She had—almost—kissed him in return; had been stirred to her depth by an ache to surrender to his touch. And had to—*had to!*—deny even to herself that she had suffered anything at all.

CHAPTER FIVE

JULIET hadn't meant to reclaim her car until her next sales trip to Munich, but on the evening of the public holiday Ilse Krantz rang, suggesting she drive her the next morning, when she would be going in to the city herself.

For Juliet it should have been a day at her desk and in the workshops, but though she was surprised by the offer, she could hardly refuse. She thanked Ilse, and the arrangement was agreed.

Ilse's car was a low-slung sports model which she drove with competent assurance. They talked about the progress being made at the Schloss, Ilse being emphatic on the subject of its old-fashioned image which she was determined to efface. In consequence Juliet felt compelled to defend it, urging the view, as she had to the Baronin, that if a twelfth-century castle hadn't the right to be old-fashioned, what had?

'*It* hasn't, if the idea is to appeal to modern tourists,' snapped Ilse. 'Satin damask curtains and antique oak are all very well, but people nowadays are prepared to settle for nylon plush and teak veneer, as long as they get a swimming-pool and regular barbecues.'

'All the same, the Baronin never seemed to lack for a clientèle until *she* decided to quit,' Juliet suggested mildly.

'A clientèle of a type, no doubt. "The old school"— the same dodderers season after season, lacking the spirit to go somewhere fresh!' sneered Ilse. To which Juliet countered,

'But wasn't it a recommendation that they did choose to come back year after year?' only to be rebuked by a scornful silence until Ilse remarked,

'You know, considering the difficulties you are trying to make for Karl, I must say he is extraordinarily indulgent of you—taking you skiing, lunching you at Die Silberkanne where everyone knows him, organising lifts for you. In fact'—appraising Juliet with a swift glance—'one wonders what special charm you work on him which the rest of us should envy?'

With difficulty Juliet contained her annoyance. She said, 'I don't "work" anything where Karl Adler is concerned. I happen to be a stumbling-block for him because I have rights that he knows he can't claim—

yet. When we went skiing, he made no secret of his having nothing better to do that day while you were with the Baronin, and his being able to give me a lift from Munich the other day was just something that happened.'

'And of course the luncheon date also "just happened"! But what about the strings he had to pull, to get you orders for your stuff which you couldn't get for yourself?' Ilse insinuated.

Juliet took that in only slowly. 'Strings?' she echoed. 'What do you mean?'

'Well, you don't imagine you'd have got straight through to Martin Bezold of Kleinmayer or sold him anything on your first trip, if Karl hadn't talked him into seeing you?' Ilse challenged.

Juliet gasped, 'But he didn't! That's just not true! He asked me which stores I had tried, mentioning Kleinmayer and another, and I told him I'd already decided to make Kleinmayer my next call. So there was no question of—of——' But there her voice trailed away as she remembered. The telephone call which Karl had gone to make before they had left Die Silberkanne! If Ilse were right, that could have been when he had prevailed on Herr Bezold to see her ... when he had interfered. If Ilse were right—and from her thin smile, it seemed that she was.

'You are saying Herr Adler told you he had had to do that for me, as well as inviting me to lunch with him, and giving me a lift home?' Juliet asked. 'He wanted you to know that he had used his influence on my behalf without letting me know that he had?'

'So you admit now that he did?'

'And chose to boast about it!'

Ilse shrugged. 'I don't know about boasting. He was

telling the Baronin about it when I happened to go into the room, and I don't suppose he was over-concerned whether you knew or not.'

'He must have known I'd resent it.'

'He probably realised you would feel so small that you would claim to resent it. Though why should you? It's only all of a piece with the rest of his gallantries towards you. Which, I ought to warn you, aren't likely to continue for too long, if you persist in the matter of your "rights". His patience isn't going to last for ever, and then——!'

'That's a risk that's always been there,' said Juliet. 'In fact, I'm as surprised as you that he and I are on speaking terms.'

'Only through his forebearance!'

'And through mine—I've had to exercise some patience too. But all the cards aren't stacked in his favour. I can play some winning ones as well.'

They had reached the outskirts of the city some time earlier, and Ilse stopped the car at the garage to which Juliet directed her. She let the engine idle and looked at Juliet in mock-pity.

'I ought to make you quote six samples of the methods you think of using. But I won't,' she said. 'I'll leave you to your dreams of beating a tycoon like Karl at his own game. But you can't win, you know. Against Karl, no one does.'

'Even with time on their side, as it is on mine?' Juliet got out of the car. 'Meanwhile——'

But Ilse cut short her thanks for the lift. 'Don't bother,' she said. 'My convenience entirely. It gave me the chance to tell you a few home truths I thought you should know. No hard feelings, one hopes?' Without waiting for a reply, she drove away.

She left Juliet seething and mortified. Home truths? In other words, threats barely veiled. Conveyed to her by Ilse as Karl's messenger, or on Isle's own malicious initiative? She had bluffed Ilse as she had bluffed Karl. But of course Ilse was shrewdly right—she probably couldn't win against Karl; she could only hope to delay his plans, and he had only to defeat her in the matter of her lease and she would be finished. He couldn't force her out of the School, but subtly Ilse had contrived to undermine her defiance of the man, and newly faintheart, she found she was doubting her ability to prod it back to life.

A twist of fate had made a girl named Juliet Harmon the enemy of a man named Karl Adler before they had been anything more than names to each other. Another twist, and they were doing battle on yet another level. At first there had been excitement to the contest. But since then a strange alchemy had been at work. Somehow, even when she clashed with him for pride's sake, her heart was not now in the fight. She would much rather have been in accord with him, and since his inexplicable impulse to kiss her out of sleep, the memory of his mouth's pressure upon her willing, parted lips, could set every nerve aquiver to the longing for his kiss to have been a lover's assertion, a lover's quest in search of a love that he hoped was returned.

But of course it hadn't been, and she couldn't afford to fantasise on the sweetness of a moment which, he admitted, had spelled nothing to him but an opportunity to be taken. And if lingering on the might-have-been of his impulse was leading her into this nonsense of apathy towards their differences, it had to stop. Instead she was going to remember how he had dared to put her under obligation to him, probably relishing a sense of power in doing it. She wasn't going to deny the possibility that he had enlisted Ilse as his deputy gadfly, and she was going to convince herself that the pull of his attraction for her was merely physical—a magnet of mere looks and voice and touch, and she had character enough to resist that—hadn't she?

Sooner than she expected, her resolve was given a fillip by an incident of a few days later, when she was to be utterly confounded by two of her workers being accused as common trespassers and thieves in the forest they had been free to range at will for years.

The two were brothers—Edmund and blind Helmut Jäger, the latter's speciality being carved animals, fashioned by the seeing eye of his skilled hands and tools out of the wood he tracked down for himself from instinct and touch and even smell, and which he was used to finding among the inevitable jetsam of the forest floor.

Edmund always went along as his guide on these forays; when no fallen log or tree-feller's rubbish took his fancy, they would mark a standing tree of birch or alder or pine; the School would put in a tender for it, and if a price were agreed, the forest-ranger would authorise its felling and sale. Much of the timber the School used was obtained so; regular parties reconnoitred the woods for their raw material—lime and beech and birch and cherry—and hitherto, even in Grandpa Weisskop's long memory, no one had ever barred their way.

But Edmund and Helmut, searching in the area leased by Adler Classics, had been apprehended and warned off by Karl's felling foreman. Aggrieved and

dismayed, the brothers brought their dilemma to
Juliet. Never before had they been accused of trespass,
never before forbidden to glean the scrap timber they
needed. What was more, much of the beech and maple
which the School used in bulk grew in that area. Were
they not to be allowed to mark it down for purchase as
they had always done?

As indignant as everyone else, in all justice Juliet
had to point out that the standing timber no longer
belonged to the Baronin, and Adler Classics had a right
to choose its customers. The foreman must have been
acting within his orders, but though there was no
doubt as to who had given them, the accusation of trespass for mere gleanings, that was not to be borne!

She soothed Edmund and Helmut as best she could
and telephoned the Baronin, who was sympathetic but
was powerless to take sides, pointing out that the timber was no longer hers to sell or to withhold. And as for
trespass, the law on that wasn't too well defined, was
it, she appealed.

'In England, damage to property has to be proved,'
Juliet pointed out.

'Here too, I expect, dear. But your man of business
could advise you. Or would you like to consult mine?'

'I'd prefer to tackle Karl Adler first. Would you ask
him to come to see me, Magda, the next time he is
over? If he has a case against us, I'd like to hear it, and
to put ours,' said Juliet. She had known Magda
couldn't help, but she had needed a listener for her
rancour, and she had Magda's promise to act as her
messenger to Karl. Before they had rung off Magda
had urged, 'Try not to antagonise him, Julie. I'm sure
he likes you and wants to make a friend of you.' To

which Juliet had replied non-committally. With Karl
Adler as a friend, who needed enemies? she had been
tempted to ask.

Without warning her of his arrival he came down to
the School a few days later. At the time, she and Wilhelm were out in the stockroom at the far end of the
building, checking a consignment of varnishes, sand-
papers and solders which had just been delivered.
When she came through to the main workshop he was
there, oblivious of her approach, so intent was he at—
of all places!—Helmut's bench, watching Helmut at
work on a larchwood crocodile, scaly and grained, and
taking its final polish. Nearby on the bench was a
'woolly' sheep, awaiting the insertion of its ears, a
menacing bull, a haughty llama and in Karl's hand a
dozing cat, neat and collected, paws folded under.

He continued to talk to Helmut, and Juliet, conscious of her dungarees and a shirt stained with linseed
oil from a defective can, deplored the prospect of an
interview thrust upon her at such little notice that she
hadn't rehearsed it and knew she was looking like a
garage hand who had just eased out from under a car.

But there was no escape. Other people had noticed
her, and Karl was turning. He put down the cat, offering his hand. She didn't care at all for the glint of challenge in the blue eyes, nor for having to wipe her own
hand on the hip of her dungarees before she could
decently take his.

His smile was audacious, assured. 'You wanted to
see me? Shall we talk?' he asked.

'Yes, but not here.'

'And not, I hope, until I've accepted an invitation to
see your people at work, which I don't seem to remember you've issued?'

'I'm sorry, I hadn't realised you'd be interested,' Juliet said stiffly.

'Surely? On a broader scale, I'm in the same line, aren't I? Do you sell any of your stuff on the premises?'

'To any visitors who want to buy, yes.'

'Good.' Karl turned to touch Helmut on the shoulder. 'I like your cat,' he said. 'How much is she?'

It was Juliet who told him and he laid the appropriate notes on Helmut's bench, then moved on to the next to handle and ask questions and appraise, reminding Juliet inevitably of Royalty on an industrial tour, gracious and interested and welcomed.

Which latter, in his case, was odd. Everyone knew him and the threat he embodied; some of her workers probably guessed why he was there. Yet there wasn't one of them who didn't seem to warm to his attention, basking in his respect for skill, telling him all he wanted to know.

Going over to the enemy, were they? Juliet watched and listened jealously, though only too conscious of the times when she hadn't been proof against his charm herself. Even now ... even now, moving at his side, hearing his voice, she was acutely and vividly aware of her exposure to him, as to the peril of a flame from which she ought to step back and could not. If she couldn't resist him, how could she expect them to? But they ought to, and so ought she. And *meant* to!

He brought his cat with him when he went through with her into the house. Fitting the cat's smooth contour into his palm, he commented, 'Deceptively cosy-looking creature, isn't she? Eyes closed, claws sheathed. Pounce upon a victim? Nothing further from her mind!' He paused, frowning in a perplexity which couldn't be genuine. 'Reminds me of someone. Now who?'

Juliet said, 'I'm sure you know whom you mean, and you intend that I should. So let's leave it there, may we?'

He shrugged. 'But of course.' The cat went into his pocket and he sauntered over to a side-table to take up a wooden fruit bowl, as smooth as glass, its delicate grain a shimmer beneath its surface.

'What's the wood?' he asked.

'Ash.'

'Nice work. Whose?'

'Mine,' she said. And then levelly, 'The last thing I did under Gerhard's tuition.'

Karl nodded. 'He trained you well. You've gone on doing other things since?'

'No. I could never be more than an amateur. Now I work *for* professionals. I'm not one of them. I'm simply the manager here, as you know.'

Another nod. 'Managing some things, it seems, beyond your terms of office. I understand you take strong exception to my daring to guard my own property from possible marauders? Is that so?'

'Marauders! A blind man with his brother as guide, in search of your timbermen's leavings!'

'They were still trespassing.'

'Strictly, I suppose, yes. But by a right they've always had.'

'What right?'

Juliet shrugged. 'Habit, custom, usage. Or, if you like, Baron von Boden's blessing, which the Baronin has carried on.'

'Without its following that I need grant you the same freedoms.'

'Oh, you *need* not!' she scorned.

'And supposing I made an exception for your blind worker, what about the others? Do they also expect to roam the forest and make their selection of my timbers at will?'

'All those who, like Helmut Jäger, can tell by the way a piece of wood moulds to the hand how it will carve up and into what. They want to be able to choose their own, and for a blind man it's essential. As for their marking of suitable trees——'

'Yes, that,' Karl cut in. 'We employ selection teams too, and what if their choice of a suitable timber for felling clashes with yours?'

'Then of course their right to it would override ours.'

He sketched an ironic bow. 'You are *too* generous!'

'Not but that our money was always considered good enough,' she snapped back. 'However, my reason for asking you to see me was to find out just how the School stands in this matter of trespass, and now I suppose I know. And of course shall bow to your ruling.'

'I'm glad of that,' he agreed blandly. 'Short of erecting fences around my area of timber, how otherwise than by your compliance could I keep you out?'

'And that's your last word, is it—that we stay out?'

'Such a hardship, is it, considering how many hectares of forest there are for your roaming, where I *haven't* leased the felling rights? And you must have other sources of supply of wood than your charity pickings at my expense?'

'Of course we have contracts with other merchants.'

'Exactly. Which makes me wonder whether your claim that your particular need is for the timbers we've leased isn't your idea of a justifiable harassment. It could be, perhaps?'

She stared. 'It's true that there's more beech and pine and walnut in that area than anywhere else on the slopes. But I've never made such a claim to you!'

'No. I had it from the Baronin, pleading your case. Fair enough. But it doesn't do much for my suspicion that you could be using the fact as a form of blackmail inspired by your need for revenge.'

Juliet flared at that. 'How dare you?' she exploded, and without giving him a chance to reply, plunged on, 'And since we're being frank about our suspicions, what about mine—that your refusal of rights which the School has always enjoyed could well be your back-door method of getting your way in the bigger issues at stake? Cut off our supplies at the root, hamper us in every way you can—in other words, a cold war that could be more successful than a hot one? Slower, but equally sure in the end. Am I right?'

'If you were, should I have enquired as to your other sources of supply?' he countered. 'But your thinking it at all shows that you've a flair for malice which is at least the match of your other talents. Which, if I may say so, are not inconsiderable.'

'Thank you. Do I take that as a compliment?'

'Take it as you please.'

'I will—as a backhanded one. And talking of malice, what about yours against us?' she retorted.

'You've no proof that I've shown any. Your cold war theory is so random that it's laughable.'

'*I* wasn't laughing.'

'Nor am I—at the gall which must have prompted it. But just to show that magnanimity is my middle name, I shall instruct my foreman that my authority for his ban on trespassers doesn't in future include your people on their gleaning forays. So now can you allow yourself to backpedal on "cold war"?'

She couldn't accept this sudden change of front with any grace. She said, 'If your foreman was acting on your orders, please don't make a charity of excepting us.'

'*Ach!*' Karl's exclamation was exasperated and she shrank a little from the spark of anger in his eyes. 'And if it wasn't to coax such a charity from me, why did you want to see me?' he demanded.

'Coax'—what belittling words he chose! 'I've told you I only wanted to know where we stood. And I assure you I've no need to beg charity from you—*or* from your business friends.' She held his glance as she spoke and guessed from his slight nod that he had understood her.

'Oh, that——' he said. 'The Kleinmayer order? Who told on me, then?'

'You told Magda von Boden that you had asked Herr Bezold to see me, didn't you? And I think you telephoned him before I called on him.'

Karl nodded again. 'Guilty.'

'And you didn't tell me what you'd done because you knew I should resent your meddling with my affairs?'

'Because I guessed—rightly, it seems—that you would let your sick silly pride get in the way of whatever grains of business acumen you may have. Just as, in this latest thing, you're prepared to go back to your people to report "Nothing doing" because you are a lot too stiff-necked to accept a gesture from me?'

Her chin went up. 'They'll understand.'

'Will they?' In a couple of strides he was standing

over her, his hands clamped on her shoulders, almost shaking her. 'Understand the lie you will tell them— that my veto on their gleaning is absolute, or the truth that it's your petty conceit that they have to blame?'

'I shall tell them the truth, of course.'

'Such moral courage! The truth being———?'

She had reached a decision which surprised her. 'That—reluctantly—I've accepted your offer.'

'May they forgive you your reluctance! But—good.' He straightened, releasing her, then breathed a long sigh of mock despair. 'All these words and all this umbrage in the name of an inflated ego the size of a balloon! You know, Miss Harmon, if I hadn't the restraint of a Job, I could be sorely tempted to put over my arguments in ways you'd probably find quite unacceptable to your dignity.'

'Really?' She hoped she sounded detached. 'What kind of ways had you in mind?'

'Crude ones. Physical ones. Ways that get results equally in the nursery and the jungle.' He broke off, pointing a finger. 'The fruit bowl—is it for sale?'

She looked over at the bowl. 'No. Why do you ask?' she replied, her curiosity too much for her.

He shook his head. 'It doesn't matter—if I'm expected to make a good case of my reasons for considering buying it.'

She flushed at her gaucherie. 'I'm sorry, I shouldn't have asked.'

'You shouldn't. But you did, and as I'm not prepared to go into details, no sale—hm?'

'No sale,' she confirmed in a small voice, knowing that never again would she see or use the bowl without remembering the frost of this occasion. As usual, Karl had had the last word.

At the news that the School was to keep the freedom to range the forest Wilhelm Konstat commented a gratified 'Hmm', and it was only by a chance meeting in the village that Juliet learned the truth of the foreman's expulsion of Edmund and Helmut from Karl's land.

She had gone to the inn to order a case of cider for the School's snack counter, and the foreman, Hans Schreiber, whom she knew by sight, was enjoying his noonday Kognak at the bar. He greeted her by name, inviting her to join him, which she did, choosing a light Rhine wine at his offer.

They raised their glasses.'*Prosit!*' He asked her if all was now well in the matter of her 'comrades'' gleanings. She told him it was, thanks to Herr Adler's generosity, to which he replied surprisingly,

'*Das ist gut*. For I was to blame. I should have checked first with Herr Adler that I was to evict them on sight, instead of taking it from Frau Krantz that such was his ruling. But naturally I concluded that she knew. Who wouldn't?'

Juliet absorbed this only slowly. 'You are saying that you didn't act on direct orders from Herr Adler, but only on a message from him through Frau Krantz?' she asked.

Hans Schreiber nodded. 'So I believed at the time. After all, she is on the spot at the Schloss; he is not, and what more likely, I thought, than that she should be speaking for him?'

'Likely?' Juliet queried.

'Well, on their closeness, you understand?' The man's wink conveyed more than the words. 'But what do I find, when Herr Adler consults me? That she had no such authority from him, and even tried to deny that she had led me to believe she had!'

'But Herr Adler didn't make you take the blame for the mistake?'

'Not he. As an employer, he is iron. But he is just, and in this thing he exonerated me completely, and has since settled it with your comrades. Is it not so?'

Juliet agreed that it was, and when they parted a little later, they did so amicably. But she was left with a contradiction of relief and jealous despair that was almost unbearable.

Relief that Karl hadn't, after all, ridden roughshod over the School's privileges for the sake of the pettiness of which she had accused him. And despair that she had no weapons to use against an Ilse Krantz who had the arrogance to speak for Karl, even if she had no right. What was more, he had had only to spike Juliet's own guns by disclaiming Ilse's orders to his foreman at the outset of her challenge to him.

But he hadn't done it. He had argued and defended his position as if it were his alone. Not by a word had he betrayed Ilse's part in it. Why not? There was only one answer to that, Juliet told herself. He was so much in thrall to Ilse that to shield her was more important than to make a case for himself. And Juliet's hatred of that thought was a jealousy of Ilse's power with him which nagged like a physical pain.

It was ludicrous to picture his ever threatening to deal with *Ilse* by methods she wouldn't like! Ilse would only laugh in his face and dare him to try it. Whereas a Juliet Harmon who had begun to write her own doom with him when she had rejected Gerhard Minden was never going to be allowed to acquit herself of that guilt.

A few days later she was invited by the Baronin to a party to mark the hotel's re-opening under Ilse Krantz's management. There were already enough guests in residence to make it a gala occasion of dinner, a floor-show and, if the weather were kind, a cruise by launch on the lake.

'Don't drive up,' Magda advised. 'Someone shall come down for you, and if the cruise is possible, there will be plenty of spare seats in the cars going down to the shore. And Karl Adler, who will be staying the night, can see you home afterwards.'

Juliet accepted, with the mental reservation that if it had been Ilse who had asked her, she would have found some excuse to refuse. But saying No to Magda would involve her in explanations she didn't care to make to Magda's kindly assumption that the tensions between her and Karl were slackening with time. She had to go, and wouldn't have been entirely honest if she had denied a dangerous urge which didn't want to say No. Besides, salt rubbed upon a wound was supposed to be curative, wasn't it? And there should be plenty of salt for her, in seeing Ilse and Karl intimately together.

She debated what to wear. Certainly not the brown velvet which had evoked Ilse's snide apologies for her own under-dressing. And a formal dinner, a floor-show and possibly dancing, combined with a late night cruise on the water, posed their own problem in the matter of dress. She went to Munich to solve it, and chose a long full-skirted dress in soft creamy banlon, its plunging neckline and back offset by a detachable draped hood, which she could pull over her hair out of doors.

'The gown's simplicity is all. No jewellery, *gnädige Fräulein*!' the salesgirl advised, to which Juliet agreed, sharing the flattering pretence that she possessed a jewel-case full of diamonds and ropes of pearls from which to choose and reject.

She wondered whether Magda would ask Karl to chauffeur her both ways. But on the night, she was called for by a young man who introduced himself as Johan Seiber, a learner-designer with the Adler group, who was to be her partner for dinner.

The Schloss was once again floodlit from its court-yard, its turrets and crenellations outlined against the sky like a one-dimensional stage set; a fairy-castle back-cloth to a pantomime's transformation scene. Inside, its foyer and main rooms were massed with banked flowers, but Juliet noticed with some satisfaction that Ilse's despised potted plants were still in place, as was also the heavy dignity of the Baronin's antique walnut and oak.

Ilse, sheathed in bottle-green silk jersey, her mag-nificent hair piled high to a jewelled comb, was playing hostess to the party, greeting the non-resident guests as they came in. Karl was not with her, nor anywhere in sight as Juliet crossed to speak to Magda, holding a small court of her own.

Drinks were being handed. Juliet was soon separated from Johan Seiber; apart from a few old friends of Magda's she knew hardly anyone present, but she was quickly drawn in to chattering groups, was asked for her first name and was thereafter addressed by it, or in default of it, as *liebchen*. Looking about her and listening to the crescendo of noise, she felt she did not care too much for this sample of the clientèle Isle had attracted. Most of the men appeared too grossly prosperous and their women were too loud.

'You're being impossibly square and super-critical,' she chided herself. But to judge by the way Magda

Harlequin Romance 1451
The Arrogant Duke
ANNE MATHER

Harlequin Romance
Beyond the Sweet Waters
ANNE HAMPSON

Harlequin Romance 884
Cap Flamingo
VIOLET WINSPEAR

Harlequin Romance
Teachers Must Learn
NERINA HILLIARD

4
FREE
Harlequin Romances

EXCITING
DETAILS
INSIDE

TAKE THESE 4 FREE

Harlequin Romances

as advertised on TV

Thrill to romantic, aristocratic Istanbul, and the tender love story of a girl who built a barrier around her emotions in ANNE HAMPSON'S "Beyond the Sweet Waters"...a Caribbean island is the serene setting for love and conflict in ANNE MATHER'S "The Arrogant Duke"... exciting, sun-drenched California is the locale for romance and deception in VIOLET WINSPEAR'S "Cap Flamingo"... and an island near the coast of East Africa spells drama and romance for the heroine in NERINA HILLIARD'S "Teachers Must Learn."

Harlequin Romances...6 exciting novels published each month! Each month you will get to know interesting, appealing, true-to-life people... You'll be swept to distant lands you've dreamed of visiting... Intrigue, adventure, romance, and the destiny of many lives will thrill you through each Harlequin Romance novel.

Get all the latest books before they're sold out!

As a Harlequin subscriber you actually receive your personal copies of the latest Romances immediately after they come off the press, so you're sure of getting all 6 each month.

Cancel your subscription whenever you wish!

You don't have to buy any minimum number of books. Whenever you decide to stop your subscription just let us know and we'll cancel all further shipments.

Your **FREE**
gift includes

- *Anne Hampson* — Beyond the Sweet Waters
- *Anne Mather* — The Arrogant Duke
- *Violet Winspear* — Cap Flamingo
- *Nerina Hilliard* — Teachers Must Learn

Mail this coupon TODAY!

FREE *GIFT CERTIFICATE*

and Subscription Reservation

Mail this postage-paid card today!

Harlequin Reader Service,

Please send me my 4 Harlequin Romance novels FREE. Also, reserve a subscription to the 6 NEW Harlequin Romance novels published each month. Each month I will receive 6 NEW Romance novels at the low price of 95¢ each (Total – $5.70 a month). There are no shipping and handling nor any other hidden charges. I may cancel this arrangement at any time, but even if I do, these first 4 books are still mine to keep.

CR 9-1

NAME   (PLEASE PRINT)

ADDRESS

CITY   STATE/PROV.   ZIP/POSTAL CODE

Offer not valid to present subscribers

Offer expires August 31, 1979

PRINTED IN CANADA

Take these 4 best-selling Harlequin Romance stories

FREE

...◀**K** EXCITING
DETAILS
INSIDE

Business Reply Mail

No Postage Stamp
Necessary if Mailed
in Canada

Postage will be paid by

Harlequin Reader Service
649 Ontario St.,
Stratford, Ontario.
N5A 6W2

Canada Post
Postes Canada

021

kept aloof in her own circle, Juliet suspected she might have felt the same.

Until shortly before they went in to dinner, there was no sign of Karl. But then suddenly he was there, elegant and assured, and her heart defied her will by quickening its pulse at her sight of him.

His height gave him precedence of the people milling near him. Above their heads he was looking about him ... carelessly over at her, and as their eyes met before they both looked away, she recalled the hackneyed lyric line—'Across a crowded room'—and recognised the strange magnetism he had for her for what it was. Against all likelihood, against all wisdom, she had fallen in love with him, and the very paradox of her weathervane feelings and actions bore it out.

She defended herself hotly because she wanted him to think her worthwhile. She fought him on issues of justice for other people besides herself, but wishing all the while that they could agree. She froze in pride when a tenderness she craved wasn't there for her ... and melted to the few generous gestures he had made her ... and froze again, because a one-sided love with no future mustn't show.

He was moving her way now, pausing to speak to people, but coming. If only, if only she had the right to run to meet him, hands outstretched——! But Johan Seiber was at her side before him, inviting her to go in to dinner.

CHAPTER SIX

DINNER was served at tables for four beneath the brilliance of crystal chandeliers to which the soft candle-glow on each table of the Baronin's régime had given place. Juliet and her partner found their cards at a table which they shared with two of the resident guests. The immediately adjacent table remained empty until, when everyone was seated, Ilse and Karl took their places at it, sharing it with no one throughout the meal.

Ilse smiled distantly at Juliet, and Karl nodded to Johan. He was an attractive youth, with black hair, velvet brown eyes and a dimpled smile. He laughed a lot and used the brown eyes flirtatiously for Juliet's benefit, and she rewarded him for trying so hard by responding as vivaciously as she could. Besides, flirting with him as if she hadn't a care in the world acted as a temporary sedative for the bruising knowledge she had just faced. And if, as she suspected, Ilse had arranged the dinner placings in order to impress her with her own charm for Karl, Juliet was not unwilling to show how little she was being impressed by anything other than Johan's lively attentions.

Unfortunately he proved to have no flair for managing his drinking. He had ordered champagne, consumed most of it himself, laughed increasingly and foolishly as the meal progressed, to the point where Juliet realised that to any onlooker, she must appear to be abetting and indulging a near-drunk man. And the one onlooker whose opinion she cared about was Karl Adler ...

At the end of dinner she was glad to escape to the cloakroom with the young wife with whom they had shared the table.

The girl sympathised, 'You've a bit of a problem with your boy-friend, haven't you? Or are you used to managing him in that kind of mood?'

Juliet said, 'He isn't my boy-friend; I was only given him as a partner for dinner. If I'm careful, I probably needn't see him again.'

'Then be careful with us, if you like,' the girl offered. 'My Bruno shall act as your bodyguard.'

Juliet thanked her. But obviously she couldn't latch on to them for the rest of the evening, and presently, when people began to dance and to group, chatting, they drifted apart. She joined Magda's party for a time; danced once or twice with strangers, and later, when Johan came in search of her for the drive down to the lake, he seemed to have sobered up.

He wasn't taking his own car. They were to go in a big hatchback with several other people, and the same crowd stayed together when they boarded the hired launch at the landing-stage.

It was a luxurious craft, dressed and lighted for the occasion; its saloons ablaze, its afterdecks discreetly awninged and dim; spacious enough for a hundred people to find themselves a lone corner or to gather anywhere without overcrowding.

It got under way to the soft strains of Viennese waltz tunes relayed from the main saloon. The Silbersee, dark and smooth, parted to its bows with scarcely a ripple and followed it with a soft creaming wake. The night air was gentle and windless; summer in Bavaria had arrived.

Juliet soon detached herself from her crowd to explore alone. She mounted a companionway to an upper deck, but found it was being used as an impromptu dance-floor, and came down again. She went to lean on the rail of a deck behind the saloon where, except for the occasional couple who strolled past, she was alone with the night and the lake and her thoughts.

But not for long. Presently there was a touch on her shoulder from a hand which slipped lower to her waist. She turned to face Johan Seiber, his encircling arm claiming her and holding on.

'Why did you run away from me?' he wanted to know.

'I didn't run away,' she said. 'You were talking to the others, and it was so hot in the saloon, I wanted some air.'

'You ran away,' he insisted obtusely. 'Not very friendly of you, was it, considering the fun we had at dinner, and all we could have before the night's out?'

'I was going back, so shall we go now?' was all she could find to reply.

But he wasn't to be humoured so easily. He was in a post-drinking contrary mood. 'Why should we, now I've found you? Besides'—pursuing his obstinate line of thought—'you *did* run away from me, don't deny it, and for that you owe me a forfeit which I'—he made a separate point of each following word—'am ... now ... about ... to ... take!'

'You are *not*!' Juliet could have given in, but she would not. She fought him, pressing down hard on the grip of his hands at her waist, as determined that he should not kiss her as he was that he meant to.

She turned her head this way and that, avoiding his lips. He had been smiling, but he wasn't now. He called her an ugly name when at last she broke free, panting, stepping back from him, her heel coming down on the foot of someone standing immediately behind her.

She turned in apology. 'I'm terribly sorry! I hadn't heard——'

'Don't mention it.' She had sensed who it was before Karl Adler spoke. He looked across at Johan. 'Enough is enough of that, wouldn't you say?' he queried coldly. 'Or is it only to a common onlooker that the lady has made it clear that she is Not Amused?'

Johan muttered, 'She's a ——' Karl cut him short.

'Maybe, but a man should recognise when he's on to a losing thing. So cool it, will you, and——?' A jerk of his thumb in the direction of the saloon pointed his meaning, and with a shrug Johan took the hint.

Juliet, reaching for the hood which had slipped from her hair, met Karl's hands flicking it up and adjusting it for her. She said again, 'I'm sorry about that. I hope I didn't hurt you?'

'I shall live,' he said laconically. 'And the scene I interrupted—what was that in aid of?'

She stared out over the water. 'He'd claimed he had the right to kiss me, and I didn't want him to. It was all very—silly,' she concluded lamely.

'Even though you may have allowed him to think he had the right?'

She turned her head quickly. 'But I hadn't! I——!'

'Are you sure?'

She frowned. 'What do you mean by that?'

'That if you'd encouraged him and then turned him down, he had every excuse. Men don't take too kindly to being fooled.'

'Fooled? I *hadn't* encouraged him!' she denied.

'You surprise me. Nobody seeing the two of you at

dinner could be blamed for supposing you knew very well what he was asking of you, and that you were responding with considerable fervour then.'

'He had begun to drink too much, and I had to humour him, to play along.'

'I've been talking to him since, and he wasn't drunk. And I'd say he wasn't drunk just now. Just a shade party-high, that's all.'

'You are taking his part! You are claiming he had the right to—to maul me and to kiss me against my will?'

'*He* appeared to think you'd given him an amorous promise which you were breaking, and from all the signs at dinner, I'd be inclined to agree with him.' Karl paused. 'And perhaps I cut him short too soon. Perhaps you had asked for the shock of hearing what he thought of you.'

'He had already called me by a filthy name which I didn't deserve. And you have the nerve to defend him!' Juliet's hands, curled into fists, were at her breast, pressed there partly to control the trembling of her wrists, partly to ease the ache of a sense of injury that was almost a physical pain. She went on, 'Anyway, even if it's only a kiss, why should a man expect to take what he wants, when *he* wants it, against a woman's will?'

'Probably because Nature made him that way, and quite frequently he may only be jumping the gun of an invitation——'

She had to unclench her teeth in order to speak. 'Johan Seiber had had no invitation from me!'

'Any more, on a wider canvas and over a longer time, than Gerhard supposed he had had from you, one questions?' Karl insinuated.

She stared at him, aghast. 'You can leave Gerhard out of this,' she said, her voice thick. 'He had no encouragement and no cheap invitations from me—none! And how dare you compare him to a—a puppy like Johan Seiber?'

' "Puppy" could be right,' Karl agreed. 'But the parallel is there. At dinner you were signalling Yes to Seiber, only to floor him later with a rather waspish No. So wasn't it possibly the same for Gerhard? A man "takes" at random without much fore or afterthought. But I can't believe that Gerhard reached the point of proposal to you without your having given him *some* hope he would be accepted.'

'I've told you already, I'd given him none. And before he proposed to me, he'd hardly asked for any. It was only after I had refused him that he began to accuse me of wronging him, which was why I was forced to leave the School and go home.'

'Then perhaps his technique was at fault. Perhaps he should have "taken" while he could; cut his losses, but at least have shown you pretty forcibly what you might be missing, marriagewise.'

'I *knew* what we'd both be missing if I married him,' she said in a low voice.

'But weren't prepared to forgo it, to help a dying man?' Karl moved a step closer, covered each of her fists with a hand and drew down her arms to grip them rigidly at her sides. He said very softly, dangerously softly, 'You have no heart, have you, Juliet Harmon? Either to indulge a puppy in a few harmless kisses, or to share an unromantic year or two with a man who, as things were for him, couldn't have been a burden on you for too long? And so—do you know?—I'm inclined to treat you as Gerhard should have done—and didn't. Teach you a lesson on how, with a woman like you, a man may be entitled to "take" at his will, not hers, and without any invitation or implied promise—like this!'

He released her hands; one of his own tangled in her hair, bunching it to drag back her head. His other arm went round her, pinioned her close to him, knee touching knee, thigh to thigh, breast to breast. Beneath the drape of the hood which had fallen away his fingers explored her bare back and fastened below her shoulder-blades with bruising pressure on her flesh.

He studied her face with insolence, even contempt, in his eyes. Then, making a deliberate exercise of something which should have spelled tenderness and mounting rapture for them both, his lips took hers ... searched ... demanded their surrender without any gift of himself behind the savagery of the kiss.

Just so had she sometimes indulged wayward dreams of being taken into his arms for a love which, by some miracle, he returned. But he had nothing for her, and she had to fight a welling need to give, to respond, to yield, which threatened to betray her.

She struggled—to no avail. Karl's hold imprisoned her and when his kisses went, errant and exploring, to her throat and to the daring plunge-line of her dress, her will ceased to protest and she was all melting woman, spendthrift of passion, reckless.

He lifted his head and released her suddenly. Juliet's hands went to her burning cheeks. How could she hide from him the naked desire he had roused in her—*how*? But in self-defence she must. 'You'd warned me that in certain circumstances you could be crude,' she accused him. 'But I didn't realise how crude until now. You think I mistreated Gerhard, and

—all that was designed to punish me for it?'

'Let's say I couldn't resist the urge to help you to repay something of the debt you owed him; using your own callous coin for the job, in other words. I'm right in thinking you didn't enjoy it?'

'Entirely right,' she lied.

'Good. I didn't intend you should.'

She stared in disbelief that none of her sincerity had got through to him. 'I think you hate me, don't you?' she asked.

'I hate jilts——'

'I *never* jilted Gerhard! I never gave him *any* promise, any hope!'

'—and stone-hearts, in that order. Take your pick,' he finished, then took her by the elbow in a prison warder's grip.

'I'm going to return you to so-called civilisation. It could be safer for us both,' he said as he moved with her towards the saloon.

Juliet was silent, scorning to ask him what danger he could possibly suppose *he* was in.

When he left her inside the door of the saloon, she watched him join a table where Ilse was sitting with another couple. Then she went to the cloakroom, which was empty. She sat down at a mirror, going through the motions of combing her hair and renewing her make-up while the fret of her thoughts belied every calm movement of her hands.

She remembered Magda's promise that Karl should see her home after the party. Impossible now that he would either agree or offer. After this, he could not want to see her again tonight, any more than she could bear to have to speak to him. So before the question arose, she would have to find her own solution to that one.

And later? The future ahead when, from time to time, they would have to meet with reasonable decorum, while each must be remembering the raw aggression with which he had treated her tonight? How were they to carry it off? How was *she* going to react to him, torn as she was between the magnetic spell which her will could not control, and the knowledge that, since with every word and action he had wronged her, she must keep her self-respect inviolate from him? He mustn't be given the chance of such abuse of her again. At all costs, she must keep her distance from him; force him to keep his.

But there was no foreseeing nor rehearsing of that. It would have to be played out as it happened, and meanwhile there was the rest of this traumatic evening to face and, not least of her problems, Johan Seiber to avoid. Or would he be just as anxious as Karl must be to avoid *her*?

At the door of the cloakroom on her reluctant way back to the saloon she met Ilse and another woman coming in.

Ilse stopped her. 'Oh, there you are! Not having to play wallflower, surely?'

'Just doing some running repairs,' said Juliet evenly.

'Yes, well—Karl said he had come upon you in a heavy session with young Seiber. But since then you've been missing, and the Baronin has come up with the novel idea of having the launch put in at your quay before it crosses back to ours, and asking you to open up the School, so that the guests who've never seen it can look over it. She is waiting to see you about it in the saloon.'

'I'll go to her.'

Juliet found Magda anxious that she should agree. 'It could mean some valuable publicity for you, dear,' she urged. 'Apart from that, the School is a unique feature of the Lake which people ought to see. So if we put in there, with the idea of your showing them around it—would you?'

Juliet demurred, 'The workroom may be pretty untidy—the tools that are going to be used again tomorrow left all over the benches.' But at the back of her mind she was realising that the plan could solve her most immediate problem. When she had shown the party over the School and they had re-embarked, she would be on her own doorstep, and as long as she took her polite leave of the party's hostess—she wasn't quite sure whether it was the Baronin or Ilse—surely no one could take it amiss if she stayed where she was? By the time the launch had crossed the lake and the cars had returned to the Schloss, the time would be nearer one o'clock than midnight, and the party must soon break up.

She told Magda she was fully agreeable. Magda murmured, 'I'm glad, though Ilse didn't seem to think it a very good idea.' To which Juliet's unspoken retort was, 'Oh, she *didn't*?' and a determination to do her very best by all the School had to show.

The launch changed course, and on the short trip to the Rutgen pier, she remembered the two standard lanterns at either side of the main door and the looped chain of fairy-lights, used only on gala occasions, which lit the façade and were switched on from inside the building. She stationed herself by the rail and when the launch juddered to the quay, she asked the people near her to wait for a few minutes, and stepped

alone on to the jetty and along the short path between
it and the School.

She used her key on the main door, switched on
every light there was and looked into the workroom
where, as she expected, there remained a clutter of
tools and half-finished carvings on the benches. But it
was a workmanlike untidiness and there was neither
sawdust nor a curl of wood-shaving on the floor which,
by her cast-iron rule against the hazard of fire, was
swept as it always was before the workers left for the
night. The stockroom was tidy and the snack-bar was
neatly shuttered.

She had told the launch-party to take as their signal
the switching-on of the outside lights, and now they
were trooping along the narrow path in twos and
threes, and lingering outside to admire the fine wood-
work of the façade and the long shimmer of light cast
by the lanterns across the surface of the lake.

They crowded in, not all of them at once, for there
wasn't room. They looked and handled and questioned
— What number of people did the School employ?
How did they learn their craft? Very much a father-
and-son tradition, was it? Was there good money to be
earned, once a man was skilled? And was there any
future for it in these mass-produced days? For instance, if it weren't tourist-supported, mightn't it die
overnight?

The last query Juliet answered with a bland, 'But it
is tourist-supported, and fortunately the tourists, like
the poor, are always with us,' which raised a laugh at
the expense of the question, which was as regularly
asked as were most of the others put by visitors being
shown round the School.

Usually of course Juliet hadn't to do the tour-

guiding alone, and without Wilhelm Konstat or someone else to take on part of the crowd, she felt harried
but at the same time stimulated by its interest. She
explained and demonstrated and talked and wasn't
really tired. But if only it weren't quite so hot in
there! Finding herself with her back to a lattice
window, she unlatched it, flung it wide and while the
people near her were handling and admiring some of
Helmut's animals, leaned back against the frame,
grateful for the flow of cool night air.

Outside a couple were standing, close under one of
the lanterns. Leaning back further, Juliet glanced
along the line of her shoulder, recognising Ilse but not
the man. Ilse was speaking and Juliet was listening. Ilse
was saying,·

'Yes, of course. Charming and in-character and
folksy—all that, I agree. But it's nothing but a cottage
industry, only fit for peasants who until now have had
nothing else open to them. And yet this English girl—
this protégée of the Baronin's—won't admit that its
days are numbered, though it can't be long before she
finds herself without any workers to manage. What did
you say?'

Juliet did not hear what the man replied, but Ilse
answered him, 'Well, she may keep the lame and the
halt, but the able-bodied ones are going to be tempted
by the wages they can earn with Adler Classics. Karl
Adler knows that *must* force her out.' Ilse paused as
her companion spoke again. Then—'A pity? A loss
to the Lake? A bit ruthless? Well yes, perhaps. But
necessary, as Karl sees it.' She drew her lace wrap
round her shoulders. 'So if you've seen all you want,
shall we make our way back to the launch?'

Juliet straightened, slamming shut the window. So

that was it! As if she couldn't have guessed! So far, only two of her people had been bribed to leave, but if the price went up——? Very cunning! Very subtle! Given a month or two of attractive offers to the men as timber-fellers or cabinet-makers, and the School could become an empty shell where nobody wanted to work. And to hear its doom predicted by Ilse Krantz, confidently speaking for Karl, was *too* much! Juliet had to force herself to concentrate upon a woman who was fingering one of Helmut's dachshunds.

'You would like to order a pair of those? Certainly,' she smiled, outwardly calm, though inwardly raging.

She had heard from someone in the launch party that Magda had stayed on board, which decided her to make her excuses later by telephone, rather than risk being pressed into returning to the Schloss if she went to the landing-stage with the others.

They drifted off in twos and threes, and by claiming she had something to do in the house, Juliet was able to watch the last of them disappear in the direction of the jetty. She went through the routine of switching off the lights the full length of the building—the stockroom, the workshop, the outside lanterns——

But with a finger on that switch, she paused. The main door was still open, and under one of the lanterns stood the cause of the need for her elaborate ruse to avoid him—Karl.

'Wh-what do you want?' Shock put a stammer into her voice. 'I didn't realise—— I thought you'd——'

'Gone with the others?' he finished for her. 'Not when I saw you didn't mean to. Being curious enough, that is, to wonder why?'

'It didn't seem worth it at this hour, when the party must soon be over.'

'All the same, rather rude to your hostess to opt out without so much as a "Thank you for having me", don't you think?'

'I'm going to telephone to explain. Later, when they've got back. When I'm alone,' she added pointedly.

'Your reason being your fear that the Baronin might rope me in as escort to you for your trip back?'

'So if you know why I did it, why give yourself the trouble of staying behind to ask me why?'

'Then that was it?' He nodded maddening satisfaction, goading her to snap,

'Well, what do you suppose, after the way you had abused me? That I'd be all welcoming gratitude at being so honoured? If I had gone back with the others, I'd have walked home, rather.'

'As I'm going to have to walk back now.'

'By your own choice. You didn't have to miss the launch, merely in order to gloat over the effect of your insults!' she retorted.

'And you don't have to assume that gloating was my only reason for staying behind.'

'What else? You've admitted it. And you can hardly pretend, can you, that you wanted to smoke a pipe of peace with me?' she jeered.

Watching him, she was unprepared for the ironic lift which twisted his mouth. 'At this hour? Entirely unchaperoned?' he enquired mildly.

'Well then——?'

'Well then'—he echoed, the half-smile gone— 'switch off your lights, lock your doors and go to bed. And don't bother to thank me for having flushed out your unwelcome suitor before he had the chance to pester you again, which I take it you wouldn't want? So—goodnight.'

She stared at him. 'No—— Wait! You mean—that man, Johan Seiber——?'

Karl nodded. 'With roughly the same idea as mine—to let the launch leave without him.'

'And—and come back here?'

'Feeling he had a score to pay, I imagine.'

'And you got rid of him?'

'Saw him safely aboard, yes. Judging, on earlier showing, that you might find me and my gloat preferable to him with reprisals on his mind. Right?'

She bit her lip. 'Of course. Thank you——'

'And so——' Karl reached inside the door to flick the lantern-switch just above her head. As his hand dropped from the switch he allowed his fingers to trail her cheek.

'You are your own worst enemy, Juliet Harmon—do you know that?' he said. 'But at least, in coping with me, you've played safe this time. Between you and me, no dire designs on your virtue either intended or entertained—huh?' And then, out of the darkness, she heard, 'Goodnight again to you,' and he was gone.

Had he dared to laugh as she shut the door on him? After the way he had treated her on board the launch—had he *dared*? She believed he had.

CHAPTER SEVEN

WHAT was it possible to make of the man?

After accusing her of having given Johan Seiber the right to pester her, he had taken it upon himself to avenge Gerhard by deliberately raping her will to surrender to him which—did he but know!—was his to command, if only he had asked it of her in love.

He had admitted hating what he thought she stood for, so why this later unexpected overture to protect her? Scorn then; concern now—for someone who had mere nuisance value to him. Why did he bother? Because he knew by now that injustice and indebtedness to him got equally under her skin, and he savoured the spectacle of her reaction to both? Wretchedly Juliet supposed that had to be it. And the next time they met, would Karl be wearing his chivalry hat or his judge's wig? And how was he thinking of her as he trudged up to the castle in the darkness of the tortuous forest paths? With malice or with kindness? Or not thinking of her at all?

She telephoned the Schloss, leaving a message for Magda to be told why she had stayed behind. Then she went to bed, making a conscious effort to put the events of the evening—*all* of them—out of her thoughts. But when she slept she dreamed that she stood alone in the School workshop; the floor a litter of débris, the work-benches empty of tools; nobody else within sight or sound, and the dream jerking her out of sleep, back to the memory of her eavesdropping on Ilse, that willing Cassandra, prophesying the doom which Karl had in store for Magda's 'English protégée'.

Of course Ilse had warned her, though without spelling out so directly his plans for gaining his ends. When those two wood-carvers had left, Wilhelm Konstat had voiced his fears, and she had had her own. And now Ilse's news had made the threat a real one. *That* was how he meant to flush out the enemy—with bribery and tempting conditions of work. No wonder he could afford to make that quixotic gesture to Helmut Jäger and the others; he wouldn't have to give them the freedom of the forest for long, once he had milked the School of all its workers, barring Helmut and Grandpa Weisskop and perhaps Wilhelm. For could she count even on Wilhelm's loyalty, in face of Adler Classics' inducements?

In the morning Juliet tackled Wilhelm head-on. Did he know of any approach to their workers, and if so, what form had it taken?

Wilhelm did not, but pressed, admitted that he had heard 'murmurs'.

'About what? From whom?' Juliet demanded.

'From some of our own people. At the *Wirtshaus* they see how much the strangers are able to spend, and I think they begin to ask questions,' Wilhelm said.

'Questions—of the timbermen?'

'More of themselves—whether they owe it to their wives and families to go after such pay, if it is there to be earned.' He raised faded blue eyes to meet Juliet's. 'I have even thought that way myself now and then.'

'Oh, Wilhelm——!' She felt betrayed.

He beamed, paused and then surprised her with the triumphant English of a phrase he must have copied, parrot-wise, from her. 'Not to worry!' he said, and reverting to German, 'When I ask myself such questions, do you know what I reply? I say, "Wilhelm

Konstat, you are a fool. An old fool of a dog who cannot be taught new tricks. You are a wood-*carver*, not a hewer of planks. Stick to the trade your father taught you, and his father taught *him*, and let's have no more of this nonsense." That is what I say, Fräulein!'

'Oh, Wilhelm!' she said again, but this time with a shaky laugh. 'Though can we be sure any of the other men will think that way?' she demurred. 'Ought I to get them together and talk to them, do you think?'

'Put it into their heads that because they can perfect a model by shaving a millimetre off it they can manhandle a tonne of timber into chains and see it away? Hmm!' Wilhelm scorned.

'They might know they couldn't, and wouldn't want to. But they could go into Adler Classics factories as cabinet-makers or something,' Juliet protested weakly.

'Indeed so—*if* you suggest it to them, Fräulein. But if you listen to me, you will hold your tongue. It will be time enough to fight Adler when any more of our people ask for their cards,' was Wilhelm's advice.

'Or the lot of them do—to a man!'

'That you must handle when it happens,' said Wilhelm. 'In the meantime, appear to know nothing, but keep your pretty ear to the ground.'

Reluctantly Juliet had to agree that he was probably right.

The next day was Sunday, when all Rutgen flocked to church in its best clothes, summoned by the church tower's tinny bell. That is, all the mothers and fathers were in their traditional garb; the women in gold-braided aprons over dirndl skirts, silk kerchiefs and silver jewellery, the men more sombre in greys and greens relieved by quill-embroidered belts, with chamois brushes adorning perky hats. But their sons

and daughters who meant to pair off after church and
had parked their mopeds and their high-powered
motor-cycles in readiness on the village square were
all in the current uniform of youth—denim jeans and
patched shirts, boots to their knees, and not the vestige
of a hat between them.

But all the girls donned cotton lace mantillas before
going into church, and Juliet, dressed like them in
slacks and shirt, did the same. Afterwards she was
going to take herself on a walking picnic. She needed
to think, and she could do it best up there in the high
woods, alone.

She left the village soon after noon, her objective a
forest clearing almost at the limits of the von Boden
land. From lake level it was a long steady climb, taking her higher still than the Schloss. There was a road
fit for motor traffic, but she chose the century-trodden
paths, dappled by light and shade and slippery with
the gnarled air-roots of the trees.

She came out on to the clearing, hot and a little leg-
weary. But the climb had been worth it. The clearing
was a plateau of about a quarter of an acre, with
further heights beyond it and a steep drop from its
level, from which the roof of the Schloss could be
glimpsed through the trees and there was a glint of the
blue-green of the lake water lower still.

Juliet stood, looking down and up and thinking as
she had often done before what a perfect site for a
house the plateau would make. In imagination she
sited the house with its face to the view of the lake, its
back to the shelter of the mountains; remote enough
if that was what you wanted, but, by the road, within
a few kilometres of civilisation. Ideal.

She sat down in the shade of a spreading beech and

unpacked her lunch of crispbreads spread with pâté, a carton of salad, some slices of buttered yeast cake and a flask of fresh orange juice. As she prised open the salad carton she heard the distant sound of a car labouring up the steep road. Shortly below her clearing the road branched to join a main highway lower down, and she waited, listening for the change and recession of the sound as the car took that way.

But instead it came on up the rutted dead-end track to the clearing, its wheels skittering loose shale like pistol shots. Its bonnet appeared between the trees, it lurched on to the level of the clearing and stopped. A man in a tweed jacket and shorts got out, reached back into the car for a clip-board, turned and saw Juliet under her tree, and after a moment's hesitation, came over.

He was young and plump with short brown hair cut *en brosse*. He bowed to her with almost heel-clicking formality. 'Fräulein'—he said—'I hope I don't intrude?'

Fleetingly her thoughts went back to the last time a man had 'intruded' in much the same way, that time with the brash assumption of a welcome ... 'Of course not,' she said, smiling, though her look must have conveyed a question as to why he was there, for he offered his hand. 'Hermann Brentl,' he announced. 'I am an architect, and I'm meeting a prospective client here.' He glanced down at the napkin on which the food was spread. 'But don't let me——'

He broke off at Juliet's startled echo of '*Here?* You have a client who wants to build here? But this is part of the Baron von Boden's estate!'

He nodded. 'Exactly. But my client has reason to think he may be able to buy, if I approve the site.' He looked about him. 'Which, on a very cursory survey, I think I may.'

Since he was so free with his business, she decided to learn more. 'For a house?' she asked.

'A country house, yes,' he said, and when she laughed, 'You find that amusing, Fräulein?'

'Not amusing. Only—odd.' She explained, 'You see, I'd just been planning the ideal house here—how it would face, and the view it would have. And then you—— Well, that was why I laughed—at the coincidence of it all.'

'And you laugh charmingly, Fräulein.' He glanced at his watch. 'I overjudged the time it would take me to drive out from Munich, and I am far too early for my client. But please don't interrupt your meal, Fräulein. I shall go and wait in my car.'

All this earnest punctilio! thought Juliet. Besides, she had more questions to ask. 'Please don't,' she invited. 'Won't you join me? It's only a picnic snack, but——'

'Charmed, Fräulein.' More invisible heel-clicking and he sat down cross-legged, and accepted a crispbread and a plastic cup—the only one—of juice. Never mind, she had a drinking straw.

'About this house——'

'You are of the von Boden family, Fräulein——?'

Their voices had clashed, and it was she who answered his question. 'Oh no,' she said. 'My name is Juliet Harmon. I am English. Couldn't you tell from my accent?'

'Yes. There was something about it,' he admitted. 'But you live around here? On the Lake perhaps?'

She told him where and what she was doing, then returned to her own curiosity. Hermann Brentl's 'my client' couldn't be allowed to build *her* house without owning up to his name! She said again, 'This house— would you be breaking a confidence if you told me for whom you'll be designing it, if you do? I'm a friend of the Baronin's, and I may know him, you see.'

'Nothing more likely, I'd say, and it's no secret. Thank you——' Her companion accepted another crispbread. 'He is Karl Adler of Adler Classics, and through Baronin von Boden, you would know him, of course?'

'Herr Adler?' But her echo held little surprise. By some quirk of intuition she had known what the answer to her question might be. 'Yes, I know him,' she said. 'He has the felling rights of the estate, and he is building chalets for his workers. But I hadn't heard he was planning to build here. For himself?'

'Yes, as a second house to his apartment in Munich. As a leisure place for weekends, or perhaps with a view to his marrying. And you wouldn't have heard anything, as he will only buy on my approval of the site and a satisfactory land-survey report. It is all still at the discussion stage.'

Which explained to Juliet why Magda had told her nothing about the proposed sale. Meanwhile her immediate need was to pack up and get away before Karl arrived to keep his date with Hermann Brentl, who hadn't said just how early he himself had been for it, and who was working a steady, leisured way through the food.

The crispbread and the pâté were finished; he had made a separate course of his salad and was about ready to start on the *Stollen* cake. Juliet watched him in a fever of urgency. Since she had invited him to eat with her, she could hardly begin collecting cutlery and

folding cloths until he was ready. Heavens!—after
an arch, 'No really, Fräulein——' he was now em-
barked on a third buttered slice, and there was the un-
mistakable sound of a second car coming up the
gradient of the road.

Her guest heard it too, but he finished his cake,
brushed himself down and stood. 'You have been too
kind, Fräulein!' He bowed to her and went to meet
Karl, hand outstretched.

Juliet was kneeling, busy with the picnic débris, and
though she did not look up, she felt Karl's critical surprise coming over to her in waves.

Hermann Brentl was explaining, 'I arrived too early
for you, my friend. But Fräulein Harmon, whom I
found picnicking here, asked me to join her, and I
accepted——'

To which Karl drawled, 'Indeed? And I'd meant
to take you back with me to lunch at the Schloss,' and
then with direct irony to Juliet, 'You know, I have to
wonder just what our friend here has got that I
haven't?' Taking it for granted that she would know
what he meant, she thought. As she did.

She said with pointed emphasis, 'I *invited* Herr
Brentl to share my lunch.'

'That's the comparison I'm making. We both cast
a covetous eye on you—I mean, of course, on your
picnic hamper—and he gets favoured, where I didn't.'
Karl explained to the other man's puzzled glance,
'Miss Harmon and I are recalling a certain occasion
when I tried to gatecrash her picnic and didn't merit
an invitation. So what hidden attraction or influence
have you? I ask myself. Or'—he turned again to Juliet
—'is it that the lady very, *very* occasionally allows herself a melting mood?'

She did not reply, but went on collecting and stowing into her rush basket. Hermann Brentl chuckled, 'To hear you, one could well accuse you of jealousy, Adler!'

'In the circumstances, haven't I every right to be jealous?'

'Of having missed an excellent picnic? Or of my obvious success with Fräulein Harmon?'

Still looking straight at Juliet, Karl said, 'In front of her, you'd hardly expect me to be churl enough to say "Just the lunch", would you?' Then he added abruptly, 'Well, to business. What do you think of the prospects?'

'Of the site? With reservations, excellent for your purpose, I'd say,' Brentl said.

'What reservations?'

'Among them, that you aren't going to be asked an exorbitant price to get it.'

'For anything I want badly enough, I'm willing to pay whatever price is asked,' Karl snapped.

'Tenacious man,' was the architect's dry comment.

'Single-mindedness is all. It gets one there in the end. What else?'

'The land must stand up to an exhaustive survey.'

'You'll lay that on?'

'As soon as you can give the green light to go ahead.'

'And when I've passed your designs, how long before building can begin?'

'Within a few weeks.'

'And completion—when?'

The architect shrugged. 'Nine months, a year. It could depend on the winter we get. Had you any particular target date in mind?'

'What do you mean?'

'Only asking whether you're a free agent, or whether there may be a "little woman" in your background, egging you on to build her a nest!'

'Not funny. I'm unencumbered,' Karl scowled.

'All right, keep your cool. Just one of the hoarier jokes the profession trots out for clients,' Hermann Brentl soothed goodnaturedly.

'Well, if that's a sample, spare me the rest,' snapped Karl. 'And now can we discuss a few details? That damned cart-track, for instance. Where would you bring in a proper approach?'

The architect produced his clip-board and they moved away talking, giving Juliet her chance to escape. But as she was ready to leave Karl called back to her from where they were standing, 'May either of us give you a lift back?'

'Thank you, but I'm not going back just yet. I'm walking on,' she said.

'A pity. I was hoping to get your reaction to my building myself a house on this site. How would you view the idea?'

'I think it's an ideal spot,' she said carefully.

'You wouldn't consider I was desecrating the landscape?'

He couldn't really want her opinion. He had deliberately trapped her with her own words. 'That was in reference to your plan to put a sawmill on the very lakeshore,' she retorted. 'A house in this seclusion would be quite different.'

Karl said, 'Good. I breathe again,' and as if he sensed a tension he didn't understand Hermann Brentl attempted mediation.

'You could do worse, Adler,' he said, 'than to consult Fräulein Harmon on your plans. Before you arrived she confessed to me she had forestalled me. She had already designed the house!'

Juliet flushed with annoyance. Now they were both making fun of her! 'That's rank exaggeration,' she told Brentl. 'I couldn't design a house if I tried. I only said I had been thinking of how best to use the site *if* I were going to build, that was all.'

He shook his head at her in mock reproof. 'A *woman*, Fräulein—and with no ideas of her own on house design. Oh, come!'

'Meaning?' Karl asked.

'That we architect boffins say we may *build* to a man's orders, but we *design* to his woman's whim. There's a difference, you understand?'

'I see. Another of the bewhiskered platitudes to which you treat your clients?'

Karl's tone had been acid, but Hermann Brentl was not to be roused. 'Not very witty, I agree,' he said affably. 'But that's the odd thing about platitudes—the duller they are, the more often they are used. And the more they are used, the truer they become by sheer repetition. It's the law of——'

But Juliet decided she had had enough, both of Karl's asperity and the other man's bland humour. Between them they had contrived to make her a kind of sounding-board for their arguments, and while she stayed there as their butt, they would never get down to the business in hand. She sketched a wave to them behind her head as she walked away into the trees, and she did not look back.

That evening the Baronin telephoned. She needed a short rest; she had found the changeover in management rather wearing, and she was going to visit her sister and brother-in-law, newly retired from Government service, in Bonn.

'I shall be away for about a fortnight,' she said, and then, 'Karl Adler tells me he surprised you and his architect picnicking together on the Fichte Platte this afternoon!'

'Making it sound as if we were on a clandestine date?' queried Juliet tartly.

The Baronin laughed. 'How thorny you are, dear, wherever Herr Adler is concerned,' she scolded. 'He only said——'

'Yes, well—*I* was picnicking. This Brentl man arrived. I couldn't very well sit there munching in front of him, so I asked him to join me, and I may say he ate most of what there was.'

'And came back here with Karl to another four courses,' Magda chuckled. 'But I feel guilty, dear, that I hadn't told you about Karl's offer for the Fichte Platte for a house for himself. It's just that I meant to tell you when it was settled, which it isn't yet, though I think it will be. I'm forgiven?'

'Of course,' Juliet assured her. 'Though I was rather surprised to hear you were selling any of the estate.'

'Just a very small slice, and Karl was so pressing and so indifferent to the cost, that I gave in. But I confess I'm a little puzzled. *I* thought he planned a kind of *pied-à-terre* for himself, as he is so often over here at weekends. But from what Herr Brentl told me today, Karl wants him to design something much more extensive—almost a family house, in fact. Far too big for a bachelor's needs, in Herr Brentl's opinion. But he did hint too that Karl could be thinking ahead—to marriage.'

'He said as much to me too.' With an effort that hurt,

Juliet added, 'It's more than likely, I suppose.'

'As you say,' Magda agreed. 'Karl Adler is far too positive and virile a character to want to ride alone all his life. And I've more than a passing idea—though I wish I hadn't—that Ilse means that he shan't.'

Juliet, listening, caught at a phrase and echoed it. 'You "wish that you hadn't" to think so? Why not?' she asked.

There was a long pause. Then Magda said quickly, 'Forget it, please. You didn't hear me say that, did you?'

Puzzled and disturbed by her friend's urgency, Juliet agreed, 'All right, I didn't hear it,' and resisted the temptation to ask 'Why not?'

Magda said, 'Thank you, dear. I had no right——' She broke off. 'I'll be in touch after Bonn,' she promised, and rang off.

Juliet was to remember well that week of Magda's absence and its aftermath. It began for her with Wilhelm's two students' announcement that their parents were withdrawing them from the School; taken aback, she was sharp with them.

'So soon after your joining it? Why do your parents want to take you away?' she demanded.

Both were weedy, callow youths of seventeen, with scarcely an opinion of their own between them. They muttered that they didn't know.

Juliet pressed, 'You *must* know. Have they plans to send you to another school? Are they dissatisfied with Herr Konstat's teaching? Or what?'

But either they really didn't know, or they weren't telling, and though she dismissed them with the warning that she must have proper notice of their going, she realised what an empty threat this was. They had not joined the School as bound apprentices, and they were free to leave at the end of any given month.

She took her annoyance to Wilhelm who, after his usual 'Hmm!' suggested that it might be as she had feared. The boys had been as dumb with him as with her, but from another quarter he had heard that they might be going to Adler Classics or elsewhere as trainee furniture-makers.

Juliet's heart sank. 'You think Adler Classics *approached* them?' she asked.

Wilhelm, however, didn't know that, and in any case thought it unlikely. On a calmer level Juliet did too. She couldn't see Adler Classics needing to send out scouts to rope in totally unskilled employees, but the boys' defection had overtones which she didn't like at all.

She hadn't expected the rot which Ilse Krantz had forecast to set in at that end of the School's personnel. When it began—if it had to—she thought she might risk the loss of some of the older men—those who, as Wilhelm had suggested, might be justified by their family needs to go for the temptation of higher pay. But if they warned her of it, she had resolved on last Sunday's picnic walk, she would move heaven and earth to keep them on the better terms she would have to screw out of the exchequer somehow. She might succeed. She might not, and there was a limit to which she could go. But she meant to try.

She hadn't, however, reckoned with defection for what looked like defection's sake, as with the two students who claimed ignorance of why they were leaving. If that kind of rout spread to the younger men she employed, some of them not long out of training themselves and not worth more than she could afford to give them, then the School *was* in trouble. They mightn't be skilled, but as a nucleus of workers, it couldn't do without them, any more than it could continue to function without the real craftsmen whom she must try to keep at all costs.

Towards the end of the week she had to begin to fear the worst, when three of these younger men, entirely vague as to their reasons or their plans, handed in their notices. The proverbial rats abandoning ship in uncanny presentiment of its sinking? Fervently she hoped not, but the fear was there.

She was looking forward to Magda's return from Bonn. Magda had promised to be in touch when she did so, and for Juliet there was something comfortingly permanent and abiding at the thought of her old friend at the Schloss, always welcoming and always to be reached by telephone.

But on the day before Magda was due back, Juliet had an unexpected visitor. It was Sunday again and she was working in the garden. She was kneeling at an overgrown triangle of rockery, poking weeds from between the stones, when she was greeted by a *Guten Tag* in a voice she recognised, and she slewed round to face Karl. If he were staying at the Schloss, he must have walked down for she hadn't heard his car.

Still kneeling, '*Guten Tag*,' she replied coolly, needing to deny the quickened beat of her pulse which the sight and nearness of him always excited. 'Did you want to see me, or were you just passing by?'

He moved a few paces forward to stand above her. 'It depends,' he said. 'To see you, if I can hope for a civilised reception. Passing by, if not. There's something I want to ask of you.'

'Of *me*?'

'Don't worry, I'm not begging hospitality this time. I've had *Mittagessen* and I don't take tea——'

Juliet bent again to her forking, stabbing fiercely at a stubborn buttercup root. 'Isn't that joke rather stale by now? You seemed to think it very funny when you first coined it, but that's quite some time ago,' she said.

He nodded agreement. 'Exactly. The promise of our first meeting mere dim history now, with a lot of water having flowed under the bridges since then, hm?'

'Quite a lot.'

'And no doubt more of the same to follow.' He watched her in silence for some minutes while with studied deliberation she went on with her work. At last on a note of irritation he said, 'Look, if it's imperative that you compete for the Green Fingers Gold Award this afternoon, please say so, and I'll call again. If not, perhaps you'd honour me with your attention. Either or—you've only to choose.'

She stirred freed soil idly with her handfork. 'Go ahead. I'm listening,' she said—and was suddenly wrenched to her feet at the compelling command of his grip upon her elbows. He turned her about, shifting his hold to her upper arms. Taken aback, unsteady, she lurched against him closely enough to feel the thud of his heart.

Still holding her, 'Do you do it *just* to annoy?' he demanded.

Purposely obtuse, 'Do what?' she enquired.

'Most things, most times we have to meet,' he said tautly.

She eased her arms from his grip. 'It's only rarely that we *have* to meet, and today it's by your choice,' she reminded him. 'You wanted to ask something of me, d'you remember?'

'I did, and do—if I can be assured of your whole ear, not merely half of it, and if I can appeal to whatever goodwill you have towards your friend, the Baronin.'

That brought Juliet up short. Discarding flippancy, 'Magda?' she said. 'You are asking me something for her? About her?'

'If you'll let me.'

'Go on, please.'

He paced away from her, hands in pockets, paced back. 'She is returning to the Schloss tomorrow, as I daresay you know?' At Juliet's nod, he went on, 'And since she has been away, Ilse Krantz has made some necessary changes in the hotel. Changes which the Baronin may not care for, but which she ought to approve in the interests of its future——'

'Just a minute. What kind of changes? Major ones? Minor? Where? How?' Juliet cut in.

'For instance, Ilse is bringing in younger staff, updating the furnishings, introducing buffet meals in place of the old-fashioned waiter service. Those dreary potted palms have gone; in future, the hotel flowers will be done professionally—and so on.'

With difficulty Juliet did not shout her dismay. 'You are saying that Frau Krantz is carrying out this— this wretched face-lift without the Baronin's knowing; in her absence and without her consent? Is that so?'

'Necessarily so, Ilse says. Persuasion and advice get nowhere with the Baronin's diehard attitudes, and myself, I'd be inclined to trust Ilse's knowledge and experience of the modern tourist against hers.'

'Oh, you would?' Juliet flung at him. 'You'd back

your—you'd back Frau Krantz against Magda's experience of the clientèle *she* cultivated and kept for as long as she wanted, and you'd encourage a mere manageress to change everything in sight without the agreement of her chief? And more than that, to do it in secret? *Would* you?'

Karl said obliquely, 'When I appoint a manager, I expect him to manage.'

'But not to override you, surely?'

'When mine is the better judgment of a given situation, no.'

'Which I'm sure you'd claim it always is.' She could not resist the sneer. 'But even if you conceded for once that he was right, at least you'd expect him to consult you, get your consent? Whereas——'

'Whereas,' he took her up, 'Ilse has acted solo, rightly or wrongly, and the consequence of that, as I see it, is where you come in.'

'Where *I* come in?'

'If you will.' He looked down into her troubled angry face. 'That's what I came to ask of you— whether, for your friend Magda's sake, you'd do what you can to soften whatever blow she is bound to suffer from all this; try to make her see that Ilse knows what she is about, and that it's probably for the best. What do you say?'

'In other words, Ilse Krantz baulks at facing Magda herself, and has roped you in to persuade me to play go-between and troubleshooter-in-chief? I *see*!'

'You don't,' he scorned. 'As usual, you see only what your stiff-necked hostility chooses to see. So you'll probably refuse also to believe that Ilse has no idea I'm appealing to you. In your view, she and I are ganging up against the Baronin and using you as a kind of catspaw in our defence. Isn't it so?'

'Well, aren't you?' Juliet retorted. 'And whether or not Ilse Krantz enlisted you on her side, the result is going to be the same, isn't it? *I* take the brunt of all Magda's dismay and impotence in face of a *fait accompli* in her own hotel, while you aid and abet and applaud Ilse for about as high-handed a bit of chicanery as I ever met. And if that can't be described as ganging up, I don't know what can!'

'Just as I don't know what there is to Ilse which arouses you to such fury,' he remarked. 'For you dislike her heartily, don't you, and I wonder why?'

'It's mutual. She dislikes me just as much.'

'Yes.'

His flat, brief agreement was a surprise. Juliet snapped, 'Oh, you know? But she keeps you wondering as to why?'

'In her case, I don't have to wonder. I think I can guess. But that's by the way. Meanwhile, can I hope to convince you that Ilse isn't trying to make you her front man to shelter her from the consequences of what she has done and means to do? She is prepared to stand by that, and all I—just I, no one else—am asking of you is that you use your friendship for Magda von Boden to ease her into accepting Ilse's better judgments, that's all.'

'Interlarding my sympathy with little snippets of advice—"It's done, so put a good face on it, Magda dear." "A manager should be left to manage, didn't you know?" Well, let me tell you—Magda has never presumed to offer *me* advice in any crisis I've known, and I wouldn't dare to do any differently by her!' Juliet defied him.

'Interlarding nothing!' he exploded. From two or

three paces away he strode to her to clamp his hands upon her shoulders in a grip which hurt. 'I give up. I quit,' he said. 'I shouldn't have expected you would listen to me. And if there's one thing I've learned about you this afternoon, Juliet Harmon, it is that you don't do anything *merely* to annoy. With anyone you count as your enemy, you act out of a sour, calculating, ingrown malice that you don't even try to resist. It probably goes too deep, anyway. It's second nature to you now.'

She looked up into his eyes, their blue now hard as stone. 'Seeing yourself as one of my enemies at the receiving end of all this venom, I suppose?' she taunted.

'Knowing *you* see me so.' His hold had tightened even further and, angry, hurt and shamed to her core, a demon within tempted her to drive him to the limit of his patience, wherever that might be.

She lifted her shoulders, braced them. 'Go on,' she urged. 'Shake me if you feel you must; if doing something physically crude is the only way you know of getting your contempt of me out of your system—go on!'

For an instant she thought she had succeeded. Instead he thrust her from him, making a significant business of dusting off his hands.

As he turned to go, 'I wouldn't stoop to it,' he said. 'Shaking is for naughty children. For a woman like you——'

Juliet watched him walk away from her. She longed to dare to answer the unspoken threat of that with a provocative 'Yes——?' which might have brought him back to her, to treat her—how? But the word was choked in her throat by the great lump which rose and throbbed there and which turned to tears; angry, humiliated tears at first, and then of utter desolation and regret.

Why, why, why? If she really hated Karl, was repelled by everything about him, she couldn't have played the vixen better. But she *loved* him! And now he had left her in no doubt that *he* hated *her*. Why, why, why?

CHAPTER EIGHT

THE Baronin did not drive her own car. When she used it one of her garden-men acted as her chauffeur, and it was so that she came to see Juliet on the evening after her return home. Usually she invited Juliet to the Schloss, and it was a pointer to her need for privacy that she had chosen to come instead to the School. She had brought Juliet a present from Bonn, a cut glass goblet with a design of vine leaves, and Juliet's delighted thanks for it went a little way towards relieving the tension of their meeting.

But the moment had to come when Magda asked the dreaded question. 'You know what has been happening at the hotel while I have been away?'

Juliet said, 'Something about it, yes.'

'How? You have been up there and seen for yourself?'

'No, I heard it from Karl Adler. He—came to see me to tell me.'

'Made a point of telling you? Why should he have done that?'

This was difficult. What was the truth of it? Had Karl really acted, as he claimed, out of compassion for Magda, or was he only Ilse's stooge? Long thought and remorse inclined Juliet to give him the benefit of her doubt. But how to justify his motives, whatever they were, to Magda? 'I think——' Juliet began.

'Just so. You need not tell me,' Magda cut in, her voice harsh with unwonted anger. 'Ilse, knowing she would have to defend what she has done, needed you to persuade me that she was right. She would not come to you herself because she is jealous of our friendship, and if you hadn't discouraged every overture Karl Adler has made you, I suspect she could even be jealous of you over him. However, she doesn't hesitate to use both him and you for her own ends. She did send him to you, did she not?'

Juliet said, 'I thought so, but when I accused him of it, he claimed she knew nothing of his coming to me. All he wanted, he said, was to believe I would help you to accept anything Ilse Krantz had done which it was too late to undo; just to be at your side, as it were. And though I was too angry at the time either to want to or to try to believe him, I think I begin to now.'

'You have changed your mind since? Why?'

'I think—because he was so angry too that he may have been sincere. He gave up, he said, meaning he gave up any hope that I would understand his reasons for coming to me. And I doubt now whether he would have rounded on me as savagely as he did, if he had been lying.' Remembering the scorn of his 'For a woman like you——' Juliet added, 'He wouldn't have dared.'

Magda sighed. 'And so you parted at cross-purposes —as usual?'

'More than that this time. This time there were no holds barred.'

'And all because of me.'

'No. Or only indirectly,' Juliet disagreed. 'That man and I have a history of antipathy that anything, *anything* could spark off. Which makes your idea that Ilse Krantz could be jealous of me really rather funny, and if she ever heard how he uses any time or attention he has given to me, it would give her quite a giggle of her own. If she wants him, she has nothing to fear from me.'

Magda sighed again. 'You are bitter, dear. But perhaps it's no wonder, and I shouldn't add to your difficulties by unloading my troubles on you.'

'But of course you should,' Juliet assured her. 'Tell me, what can you do about all this?'

'Very little, I'm afraid, except to stop the rot from going any further. What hurts and dismays me most is the length of time it must have been planned. One little fortnight! Fourteen days and nights of my absence, and my hotel's face and habits have changed out of recognition. It couldn't have been done if it hadn't been plotted beforehand. Imagine, Julie! *My* guests are expected to stand in line to choose their own food, with scarcely one knowledgeable wine waiter in sight! And there is also a newly-imported *Dirndl* of a cigarette girl with a tray on a cord round her neck, a fixed smile like a Dutch doll's and a skirt as brief as a tutu! And that is not all. There are plans for a steel band to come out on two nights a week from Munich to play on converted oil-drums, if you please, for Latin-American dancing. Ilse Krantz pours scorn. I am *altmodisch*, out of date, out of tune with the times. But so is my dear Schloss, I reply—out of date by some seven hundred years, and there is nothing, nothing at all she can do about that,' Magda concluded on a more spirited note.

'Good for you,' Juliet applauded. 'And where do things go from here? At least you can cancel that outlandish band.'

'Yes indeed. Calypsos—compared with our tradition of real music! But that is a minor problem. The major one—how do I attract and keep the kind of people who want to visit an ancient Bavarian castle because it *is* a castle and has always been someone's home, not a cross between a dance-hall, a self-service restaurant and rooms furnished with so-called "units", instead of honest tables and chairs and beds? Tell me that?'

For all her dismay Juliet had to smile at her friend's vehemence, causing Magda to smile ruefully too. 'I get carried away,' she apologised. 'Up till now I don't think I've let even you guess how much I regret having engaged Ilse Krantz on Karl Adler's advice. Almost on sight I think I sensed that her ideas and mine might prove to be poles apart. But a new lease of life for the hotel was tempting, and in his recommending her as manager, I'm sure he meant well for me. It wasn't until I had seen them together, and had learned of their earlier association, that I saw the advantage to them both of my having taken her on. That must have counted with him too—that he should have her near him if they were taking up old threads again. They were once engaged, you see, before she married the husband she divorced in America.'

'Oh——' Juliet's thoughts had flown to the photograph of Ilse on Karl's bureau in his apartment. Did it belong to that period of their closeness or to this?

There was no telling. 'How do you know?' she asked Magda.

'Karl told me himself. Just stated the fact, without any details. I don't know what conclusions he expected me to draw from it, but I do think Ilse would like to make herself necessary to him again——' Magda broke off suddenly, scolding herself, 'There! I am gossiping, and I claim to disapprove of people who do.' Standing up, 'I must go, dear,' she added.

'But what can I do to help? I want to,' Juliet urged.

'And you have, by listening to my tirade and understanding how I feel. But I'm afraid it's a problem I must solve for myself.'

'How? Could you consider breaking whatever contract you have with Ilse?'

'Difficult, and I should only find myself back at Square One—unable to "carry" the hotel alone again and with no manager. No,' Magda mused, 'for the moment I must accept matters as they are. Unless of course—yes, that might bring things to a head.'

'What might?'

'Well, if Ilse succeeded in marrying Karl Adler, she would probably graciously quit the post herself, though that also would leave me in a quandary and would be a solution I'd deplore.'

'Would you? Why?' asked Juliet dully.

'Because, whatever you may think of him, Julie dear, and whether or not he had his own reasons for thrusting Ilse on me, I *like* the man. And what's more, Julie'—Magda pointed her words with a forefinger thrusting at the level of Juliet's collarbone—'if *you* had ever troubled or had had patience enough, you might have learned to like him too!'

'Always supposing he had ever troubled or had patience enough to care a hoot whether I liked him or not. Not to mention that at the outset, he was determined not to like *me*.'

'Which I've always been unwilling to believe, as you know.'

'Because you always look for the best in people. You'd hate to admit, as I have to, that he feels he has to revenge my treatment of Gerhard Minden, and to get even with me for my defiance of him over my lease.'

Magda frowned. 'Gerhard? But that's all in the past! And about your lease, you are fully within your rights. He couldn't be so unjust! Besides——'

Juliet prompted her pause, 'Besides what?'

'Nothing. I realised that what I was about to tell you was a business confidence between him and me, and I hadn't the right to mention it yet, even to you.' Then her goodnight for Juliet was a 'Bless you, dear, for the staunch young friend you are, and don't let your prejudice against Karl Adler get you down. You could be mistaken about him, you know.'

To which Juliet returned an ironic, 'Could I?' inevitably reflecting after Magda had gone how largely the name of Karl Adler had come to dominate all their affairs—her own, Magda's, Ilse Krantz's, the School's; his influence an ever-deepening shadow on the Lake region, changing it out of all recognition.

It was a couple of weeks later that two events broke, at the outset apparently unrelated, but then dovetailing together.

The first began as a rumour but turned into hard fact—the truth of it being the news which, Magda now told Juliet, she had had to honour as a confidence earlier. But now it could come out—she and Karl, in

the name of Adler Classics, had successfully concluded the lease to him of an area of level land at the
far end of the lake from Rutgen village, out of sight of
the accepted beauty spots and vistas, for the purpose
of building—could Julie guess?—a sawmill for pro-
cessing the von Boden timber!

Juliet found herself tongue-tied. 'Then——? You
mean——?' she stammered, and had to be helped out
by Magda's gently chaffing,

'Exactly, dear! You are being so lucid! For you
are agreeing, aren't you, that Karl Adler isn't the
ravening wolf you thought him, that he doesn't plan to
raze the School or its neighbours to the ground,
that——?'

Juliet cut in, 'I—I suppose so. Or no, I don't know
that I do agree. No'—more firmly—'I'd say it's much
more likely that he has decided to give us best and
climb down; admit that we have won our case.'

She heard Magda sigh at the other end of the telephone line. Magda said, 'Very well, think like that if
you must, dear, though I shouldn't like to witness
Karl's reaction if you told him so.'

Would-be jauntily, 'You mean, if he were forced to
admit I was right?' Juliet asked.

'I mean—if you drove him to the point of having to
convince you that you have won no confrontation with
him, but that he has *given* you your reprieve.' More
gently Magda added, 'Try to believe that it is so,
Julie—if only for your own peace of mind.'

And how Juliet longed to know that in this big
issue between them Karl had acted generously, had
been concerned enough for her dilemma to decide to
solve it in a way with which she could have no
quarrel! But dared she hope so? She feared not.

Magda could only be right if, without having actually to like her, he at least respected her. That wouldn't be much—a mere crumb of reassurance. But she hadn't even that. From his first learning who she was and how she stood in his way, he had made little secret of his contempt for her. Here and there, admittedly, he had been carelessly gallant—with a gift of a little bunch of violets, by saving her from the pestering attentions of that—what was his name?—Johan Seiber. But even then he had blamed her for encouraging the tipsy lout, and when he had forcibly kissed her himself, he had done it with accusing, spurious passion; angry with her, hating and punishing her for a jilt and a cheat. He had said so, and nothing had changed or bettered for them since. No. Whatever had caused him to change his building plans, she had no reason to hope it had been out of mercy for her. Meanwhile Magda would expect her to accept the reprieve with as good grace as she could, and she meant to try—until the second happening of that week served to destroy even the little faith she had to believe that Karl meant well by her.

The new factor took the shape of a prominent advertisement in the *Gutbach Tageblatt* for a considerable additional number of men required by Adler Classics as tree-fellers and builders for the von Boden estate. Wilhelm brought the paper to Juliet, said, 'There is also a poster on the wall of the *Wirtshaus*,' and waited for her comment.

She read through the advertisement. 'They want fifty more men. That's a lot,' she mused aloud.

'For the Klinge Platte—the sawmill site. They are in a hurry. And see the wages they are offering. It makes one think,' said Wilhelm.

'You were wondering whether some of our people might be tempted? When we talked before you advised me against letting them know I feared they might leave. But oughtn't I to test what they are feeling now?' Juliet appealed.

'I know what they are feeling now. They are talking among themselves at the benches. And though some of them are fools to see themselves as timbermen or builders, money of that figure does talk, Fräulein.'

'Supposing they all went, all twenty of the able-bodied ones, what should we do? We should have to close the School.'

Wilhelm shrugged. 'They are not likely to troop out in a body. Some will take longer to make up their minds than others. Some will go, driven by their wives, some may have the sense not to go at all. But there is nothing you can do, Fräulein, unless you can match this kind of pay or better it.'

'Which you know I can't,' said Juliet. She saw it all now, and she couldn't claim she had not been warned. Karl had threatened that he had ways of defeating her; her eavesdropping on Ilse Krantz had spelled them out and her own intuition had told her they could be real.

Her outraged imagination took a wild, extravagant turn. So the School was to be smoked out, as if it were a nest of vermin! She had allowed Magda to persuade her Karl meant it no harm. But he had only been biding his time. He had changed his plans for the saw-mill site, in order to push it forward as an emergency for which the firm was prepared to pay wages out of all relation to the local rate. He had known and calculated such money's attraction for the Rutgen men, among them her workers on whose defection he was counting and would probably get.

How could he be so petty? How *could* he? Or did he hate her so much that no revenge was too mean or paltry to use against her? And how could she have betrayed her own self-respect as to think she was in love with him? Now all she wanted was the chance to confront him, to tell him she knew just what he was about, and to make very sure that, though she couldn't win, her scorn of his methods got through to him.

But for that dusty satisfaction she had to wait to see how far and how soon he was going to succeed in bribing her workers to leave her, and in the meanwhile she listened to Wilhelm's persuasion that so far the men were only talking, not acting, and that until they did, she had nothing to lose.

Patience was irksome. If the sword of Damocles of the School's fate had to fall, she would prefer it to come down with the force of a guillotine's knife. If the men meant to go, she would rather they got on with it. She *wanted* to prove her case against Karl, and it was only in the small hours, when her spirit was at its lowest and her self-doubt nagged, that her honesty faced a question she didn't want to answer—'Do you want to see Karl again in order to tell him what you think of him? Or do you want to see him again for the sake of seeing him again, hearing his voice, watching him move——?'

By day she could tell herself she knew what the answer was. By night she wasn't sure.

She had to wait until the next weekend for the first few of her workers to hand in their notices, which she accepted stoically, too proud to appeal to their loyalty alone while she hadn't the means to make it worth their while to stay. During the next week others followed, and though they had to work out the period of their notice, all the signs were that in less than a month she would have only the remnants of a work-force, if that.

That week the Baronin was away, on another visit to her relatives in Bonn; she was so much out of step with Ilse's régime, Juliet guessed, that she was thankful to escape from it. As far as Juliet knew, Karl had not been over to the Schloss since the Sunday he had called to see her, when he had left her in little doubt that he would not willingly seek her out again.

So that she was completely unprepared to be called on the telephone one morning by a woman naming herself as his secretary.

'Fräulein Harmon?'

'Speaking.'

'Herr Adler would like to speak to you. One moment, please.'

Juliet waited. Then Karl was asking, 'You will have heard that we are developing the Klinge Platte for building, no doubt?'

'Yes.'

'Well, we are having to clear it of a good deal of timber first, and as it is mostly good beech and larch, I thought I'd remind you that your workers could probably get some useful pickings there, before the débris of the felling is burnt. If you'd care to send them over, I'll have the foreman warned.'

Juliet was nonplussed. What was he up to—with a bludgeon in one hand and an apparent olive-branch in the other? In reply she said carefully, 'Thank you for remembering us, but I'm afraid the School may not be in much need of timber gleanings for its work in future.'

'Indeed? Why not?'

Considering everything, she found the smooth question provocative. 'Surely you should know why not,' she said.

'Why should I?—short of your closing down the School, of which I hadn't heard.'

'Nor, I suppose, do you know anything about your firm's recruiting of tree-fellers and builders at fantastic pay rates, which is draining the School of its workforce, and may well close it down?' she countered.

She heard his sharp-drawn breath of annoyance. 'You mean the local campaign we're running in the region for the increase in labour that we need? But how should that affect you?'

'At *those* wages, would you expect it not to?'

'But you employ a proportion of old people, the disabled, women——'

'Who are the only ones we may be able to keep when all our valuable men have gone over into your camp.'

'You are convinced you'll lose them? Have any of them been taken on by us yet?'

'No, because those who have already given me notice have still a few days of it to run. But I'm not in much doubt that most of the other able-bodied men will follow them.'

'But you have students you are training to take their places?'

'We *had* two new ones. But they left some weeks ago. They gave no reason, but I've thought since that their parents must have been a lot wiser as to the School's probable fate than I was. Oh yes, Herr Adler'—Juliet's tone deepened with wounded anger—'you warned me that you meant to defeat me and destroy the School, but you never revealed your tactics, did you, and how was I to guess how you planned to do it, until you did it *this* way, this ... this lifeblood-

draining way that you knew must succeed, as long as
you made your terms attractive enough?'

There was a silence which stretched out. Then:
'You are suggesting that we put out public notice for
labour we need in a hurry, at wages we are fully prepared to pay to get what we want, *merely* in order to
squeeze a paltry little wood-carving joint out of business? *Is* that what you think?' Karl scorned.

'You had threatened to squeeze *me* out, so what else
could I think? And I must have been the only fool who
didn't know what you were at. Other people knew or
guessed before I did—Frau Krantz, for one.'

'Ilse? Indeed? And did she confide my perfidy to
you?'

'No.'

'Then how do you know she knew?' he pounced.

She couldn't confess her eavesdropping to him.
'Never mind,' she said coldly. 'Anyway, you've got
your result, haven't you, or will achieve it, you hope?'

Surprisingly he agreed with a flat, 'As you say. The
result is the thing. And when all your employees are
working for me, and you are telling yourself that I
snatched the last crust of your livelihood from your
mouth, you might do worse than remember the rough
justice of the adage that All's fair in love and war.'

'Yes, indeed! That to you, all's fair in war—I'll certainly remember that!' she flared.

But she spoke to an empty line. Karl had already
rung off.

Juliet was tempted to say nothing in the workshops
about Karl's offer. As she had told him, their raw
material wasn't a present problem. But as she was reluctant to let it be thought that the School's future was

in jeopardy, and as she knew Helmut Jäger at least was short of the deep-grained larch he needed for his models, she gave out the news.

She herself walked over to the Klinge Platte that evening after the fellers had stopped work for the day. She was saddened by the sight of the proud beeches and slender larches which had been the day's 'bag', not yet roped and chained for carting. But better, she supposed, that trees should fall than that people's homes should be destroyed to make room for Karl's sawmill. And whether her stand had defeated his patience, or he had been generous, as Magda claimed, at least the Lakeside folk and the School had been spared that.

The first foray showed that there was a lot of good waste to be gleaned on the Platte. On most days of that week parties, among them Helmut and his guide, Edmund, went over to explore and compete for finds. The activity became a draw for sightseers too. Tourists' cars gathered, and villagers with time on their hands walked or rowed over, all agog for the free spectacle of the regimented work on hand—the roping of marked-down trees, the lopping of their minor branches, the manoeuvring into position of the hydraulic saws which had outmoded the woodman's axe, and the drama of the final warning shout of 'Timber!' which echoed back into the mountains, only to be drowned by the thunderous crash of the doomed tree as it hurtled down to earth.

It was a clear hot afternoon when Juliet walked over alone, that day's foraging party having gone ahead of her. The area of operations had been roped off for safety, but beyond this barrier cars were parked and people were picnicking on the springy turf and mill-

ing about, waiting for the next free show to be laid on
for them.

For some time nothing seemed to be happening. A
giant hornbeam had been roped and lopped in readiness for its fall, but except for an engineer taking
theodolite readings to determine the safety angle for
the fall, there was little for the crowd to watch or
speculate on, except to argue as to what the privileged
functionaries, standing about in groups inside the
barrier, might be deciding.

At last patience was rewarded. The engineer with
the theodolite reported to the operations crew; the
sawing gear was readied for action; the hauliers taut-
ened the guiding ropes and spread out beyond range,
and as the discussion groups broke up Juliet suddenly
saw that the man walking with the operations foreman
in her direction was Karl.

He wasn't looking her way, but she immediately
ducked into the crowd, threading through it and coming out near the rope barrier further along.

She found herself standing next to Edmund Jäger
who said, 'I have lost Helmut. He wandered off by
himself into that grove of larch over there. Have you
seen him anywhere, Fräulein?'

Juliet hadn't. 'How long ago?' she asked.

'Not long. About a quarter of an hour. I'm not wor-
ried. He likes to prowl about on his own, but when I
can get across there I'll go and find him.'

Edmund moved away, leaving Juliet to watch the
preparations for the felling while keeping a covert eye
on Karl. He and the foreman had halted and were
talking, the foreman gesticulating, he nodding agreement or comprehension. It was one of the few chances
Juliet had ever had of studying him without his know-

ledge. Always before he had been too soon aware and too ready to challenge her with mockery or dispute, and the only stolen march achieved by either of them had been his, when he had kissed her while she was asleep in his car and she had ached with the longing to respond.

So that now, when she had him briefly in her private sight, for all her sense of injury at his hands, her secret scrutiny of him was an only too willing admission of how he could excite and disturb her to desire. As she indulged her long, long look, the wry thought occurred that this moment of his not knowing she was watching him was a little akin to that other one. In a way it made them quits, but only in the vaguest way. *She* was never likely to come upon him asleep and unawares, and she awake and alert at kissing distance from him ... and tempted—— That was the stuff that dreams were made of—dreams that didn't come true.

Now the saws were beginning to bite. At the noise of their whirring a colony of rooks rose from their nests in the neighbouring elms, wheeling and cawing their protest. The topmost branches of the hornbeam quivered and swayed, whipping the air in a circular motion; low down at cutting level there was an angry creaking of splitting wood. The crowd seemed to be holding its breath preparatory to the ecstatic *'Achs!'* with which it would greet the inevitable crash, when into the direct path planned for the fall a lone figure trudged with blind unconcern, out of the larch thicket Edmund had pointed out to Juliet.

A great roar of 'Timber!' went up, drowning Edmund's yell of *'Helmut!'* as he dived under the rope and ran. On the instant the sawing mechanism was stopped. But too late, as were Edmund and others who dashed to cover the distance to Helmut's aid. Only two men, the foreman and Karl, were within possible reach of Helmut, who had halted, warned but bewildered by the shouting from the crowd he couldn't see.

Both men ran, but it was Karl who reached him, though without a chance of pulling or thrusting him clear of the awful threat to them both. Instead, with a single fist-blow to his shoulders, Karl knocked him to the ground and flung the whole spread of his own body on top of him, just as the great trunk measured its length on the clearing. Just escaping them with a glancing impact, or pinning them beneath its full weight? They were covered in split branches, leaves and débris, and in the first moments of the watchers' powerlessness to help them, it was impossible to tell.

But the moment passed. Help was on its way to them now. As was also hindrance from the superfluous onlookers common to any disaster. Juliet was praying, as she sensed others about her were doing also. Knowing, for all her will to run ... to run to Karl, that there was nothing she could for him, she tried to stay where she was, but was carried forward and nearer as the rope barrier went down to the great press of the crowd.

She heard Edmund's half-shout, half-sob, '*Er ist mein Bruder. Er ist blind*,' and heard people relaying the information to each other, 'The boy is blind. That is why he took no heed, his brother says.' A call for a doctor was put out by megaphone, and two men detached themselves from the crowd and ran over.

As far as was known, neither Karl nor Helmut had moved since they fell. The rubbish covering them was

cleared and the doctors knelt beside them, touching
experimentally and conferring with each other.

'They will have been knocked unconscious.'

'Their backs may be broken.'

'Or their legs or arms.'

'If they come round they will need pain-killers. Will
the doctors have them with them, do you think?'

'Not likely, if they are only out with their friends, as
we are.'

The anxious speculations went on around Juliet,
voicing her own desperate fears. Her heart was sob-
bing, 'Karl, Karl, I love you. I'll forgive you anything
... everything—for this.' And 'Greater love hath no
man——' and 'Please God, he'll never know what he
means to me, *but let him live*!'

At last it seemed, the doctors agreed the still figures
could be moved. The nearest ambulance was at
Gutbach, but stretchers of tarpaulins and staves were
improvised and carried to a drawn-up covered lorry. It
moved away, headed and followed by cars, without
much more being learned by the crowd, except the
names which were being passed around.

'The boy—Helmut Jäger. A wood-carver at the
Schule des Schnitzarbeits on the Silbersee. The other
—the hero—Herr Adler of Adler Classics, who own
the timber rights and are clearing for building here.
Yes—Adler himself. Do you hear that, Albrecht? God
send they both pull through.'

There was comparative quiet on the Platte as the
sightseers drifted away, back to their cars. But the
sounds of the work in hand began again and went on.
A hundred men could not knock off because two un-
fortunates had been injured. This afternoon's ill-

chance was a hazard of the job, and might have be-
fallen any one of them.

Juliet got a lift on the School's work-wagon on its
return journey with the gleaners' spoils of timber.
Among them were three ungainly lumps of wood—
Helmut's treasure trove of larch which someone had
found and brought away from the scene of his fall.
Juliet carried them with her when she dropped off the
lorry at a cottage on the lakeside and went to break the
news to Herr and Frau Jäger.

She stayed with them until she calculated there
would be news from the hospital, when she went to
her own quarters to ring up.

'You are a relative?' she was asked from the ward.

'No, but I am enquiring on behalf of Herr Jäger's
parents,' she said.

'His brother came in with him and is here still. But
I'll put you on to Sister,' said the voice. 'Hold on,
please.'

Juliet warmed to the quiet-voiced reassuring manner
of the Sister who reported of Helmut, 'We have him
in a single room off the ward. In Casualty he was put
under sedation for shock, and he won't be X-rayed for
suspected crushed ribs until the morning. A broken
left ankle has already been put in plaster. We are allowing his brother to stay the night, if that is all right with
his parents?'

'Yes. Yes, I'm sure it will be. I'll tell them,' Juliet
said, and then, with her heart beating hammer-strokes
in her chest, she risked a snub.

'And Herr Adler? In—in the same accident. Could
you tell me——? How he is too?'

There was a pause which made her think she was to
be refused. Then the Sister asked, 'You are the lady

who rang earlier? I didn't answer the phone myself, but—his fiancée, I think she—that is, you—said?'

His fiancée? Ilse? Claiming him? Juliet swallowed hard on her sick dismay. 'No, that would be someone else. A Frau Krantz, I think,' she said. 'I employ Helmut Jäger, but I'm only an—acquaintance of Herr Adler's. He——'

'Yes. And he came off the worse, I'm afraid. As I understand it, he flung himself on top of the boy as the tree came down, and he has spinal injuries, it is feared. But he is also under heavy sedation for the time being, and we have him here too, in a single room.' The Sister paused. 'He can't have any visitors yet, but neither of them is in immediate danger, Fräulein, you will be glad to know.'

'Oh, thank you, I *am*,' Juliet said fervently. 'And Helmut's parents will be too. They know, you see, that Herr Adler almost certainly saved his life. And could *he* be visited yet, Sister? May I tell them when?'

'Any time after tomorrow, I think. Perhaps you will ring the ward and ask?'

Juliet replaced the receiver with mixed feelings of gratitude, guarded relief and a sense of desolation which would last longer than either. Helmut was not too seriously hurt, and Karl was not on a danger list. But he was there, drugged, helpless, and possibly only through the most skilled surgery might he walk again. Ski again. Drive a car. Climb the mountain paths of the Silbersee slopes, as he had had to do on the night he——

Remembering the savagery with which he had punished her that night and then, quixotically, had taken pains to protect her, she realised that that was partly what she loved in him. It was the *enigma* of him, his dynamism in anger, his effortless charm in repose. His arrogant sureness of success; his 'common touch' with lesser folk, which she had jealously glimpsed on the day he had come down to the School and had talked with her workers. His callous destruction of her livelihood, compared with his rare, small kindnesses to her—— Yes, he was as he was and would always be, and that's how she would have taken him, troubled by him, challenged by him, enchanted in turn, if he had ever given her the chance, as he never had and wouldn't now. For now she mightn't ever see him again. Probably she couldn't even visit him in hospital, except at Ilse's indulgence, and before the autumn she would have had to close the School and go home.

Drearily she pulled herself together and went back to the Jägers with the moderately good news. Nowadays, she could tell them, cracked ribs were often left to heal themselves and an ankle in plaster meant only a few weeks on a crutch. A broken spine was something else again—but she must tone down the menace of that for their sake. They mustn't feel guilt but only the pride which she herself knew, at what Karl had done for their son.

CHAPTER NINE

Two days later Juliet drove Helmut's parents to Munich to see him. They were allowed only a quarter of an hour's visit, so she did not go with them to the ward. But they promised to bring such news of Karl as they could get, and when they rejoined her they said he couldn't be seen. He was being prepared for exploratory surgery, and the bulletin on him was the non-committal 'As well as can be expected.'

Juliet supposed that Ilse might have been given more details, and though pride forbade her begging anything of Ilse, she felt that she did owe the other woman some condolence, and rang up the Schloss.

Ilse thanked her coolly, but was discouraging of her interest.

'I hope you haven't bothered the Prinz Franz with enquiries,' she said.

'Only on the day of the accident, when I had to ask about Helmut Jäger for his people, and naturally I asked after Herr Adler too.'

'And they told you? Usually they restrict information on serious cases to relatives and—well, someone as close to the patient as I am.'

Juliet said patiently, 'Yes, so I was told, and at first the Ward Sister did mistake me for you.'

'Mistook you for *me*?' Isle's shocked echo implied that this was impossible. 'How could she?'

'Only over the telephone,' Juliet corrected. 'Apparently you had rung up earlier—Herr Adler's fiancée, the Sister said, and she supposed that I was you, ringing again.'

'Oh, I see,' Ilse accepted the explanation, confirming Juliet's fears. 'Meanwhile, I suppose you know that Karl isn't to be visited? Even by me—for the moment?

'I hadn't thought of asking to do so,' Juliet assured her. 'Though I know Helmut Jäger's mother and father will want to thank him as soon as they are allowed.'

'Yes, well—that's different,' Ilse conceded. 'And I

was only preparing you for a possible snub from his surgeons. For you have no claim on any right to see him, have you?'

'None whatsoever,' Juliet agreed. (Only love, and a charity I'd hope I'd be willing to offer *you*, if I were his fiancée and you were in my place, was her unspoken thought.)

'Well, that's how it is at the moment,' said Ilse, apparently mollified. 'I just wanted to warn you against presuming on any attentions Karl has paid you from time to time—even while you've been obstructing him all you can. Though who, after all, can blame you— totally on your own, without a man to fight your battles for you? And I promise to let you know myself how Karl progresses, when he does,' she concluded graciously.

'Thank you so *much*,' returned Juliet, hoping the irony of her emphasis found its target, but doubting it.

She was longing for Magda to come home from Bonn, but before she did, there were some inexplicable results from the expiry of the notices Juliet's workers had given her.

Usually any gossip or news reached her through Wilhelm, but this time it was his wife who reported the non-happenings which had followed the men's departure. She and Juliet were preparing the midday snacks at the lunch counter when she said, 'Heidi Boltz and Berthe Mayer and one or two of the others were saying they would like to help again here, if you could see your way to paying them a little for it.'

Juliet's smile at that was rueful. 'As if you and I couldn't manage it between us, now that we have less than half the number to cater for! But what's the idea? Aren't Heidi and Berthe and the rest still earning at the

Wirtshaus and the cafés, doing for the Adler timber-men and the builders? And they are, I know, for I was talking to Renate Müller only the other day. Anyway, I couldn't afford to pay them now for what they used to do for love.'

Frau Konstat sighed. 'No, of course not—as I told them. But it's their men, you see, Fräulein. Berthe and the others only work part-time in the village, and if they could earn the little bit more here——'

'But why should they need to? And what do you mean about "their men"? They've all left us to better themselves with Adler; their wives can't possibly need to come back here to boost the kind of money their men are going to earn! If they're not getting it already, that is.'

Frau Konstat shook her head. 'Which they are not, and are not going to, it seems. The pay-foreman is refusing to take them on.'

Juliet stopped slicing cheese, and stared. 'Not? But —Adler are still advertising for men, and ours——'

'Orders, the foreman tells them. He has his orders. Nobody to be taken on who has worked at the School during the last twelve months. He asks them, and they tell him—Boltz and Mayer and Müller and all of them, and then he says, "Sorry, man—nothing doing for you,"' Frau Konstat said.

'But they are *skilled*!' Juliet protested. 'And when they left us, they must have known they had every chance of being taken on by Adler.'

'They thought they had, and they are all fine, strapping fellows who could fell a tree as well as any who are working over there. But the foreman wouldn't say why he was turning them down; just that he had orders not to take on any skilled men from here.'

'Orders—from whom?' Juliet demanded.

'From his boss in the main Munich pay-office, one supposes.'

'And he, no doubt, from the Adler directors.' Juliet thought for a moment, then asked, 'Look, where is this pay-clerk to be found? In that chalet they call the estate office?'

'There, yes. Or in the *Wirtshaus* at *Mittagessen* time.'

'Right,' said Juliet. 'It might be easier to talk to him there, over a drink.'

'Talk to him, Fräulein?' the old woman hesitated.

'Yes. He has a perfect right to turn the men down. But I have a right, as their previous employer, to hear what he has against them. I'm going to claim the right, anyway. I'm going to see him.'

'And the men—Boltz and Müller and the others? Could you think of taking them back, Fräulein?'

Juliet said, 'Willingly. We need them. But would they want to come? Mightn't they be too proud?'

'And if they were, at that, you should let my Wilhelm talk to them,' Frau Konstat advised sagely. 'And if they wouldn't listen to him, then they'd have to heed their own Berthe and Heidi and Renate snapping the clasps of their empty purses at them. They'll listen, Fräulein. I've always had the last word with Wilhelm, though he hasn't always known it, and if any of those others are worth a bag of wood shavings, they'll get their men back here, you'll see.'

So! thought Juliet, as puzzled as she was indignant. Karl had been responsible for recruiting a work-force at pay which he must have known would attract her workers, however coldly he had denied being in competition with her. And now *somebody* above him or below him in the authority line had stepped in and refused jobs to them. Who? And why?

Her thoughts flew to Ilse, remembering how Ilse had presumed to speak for Karl in the matter of the School's right to glean from the estate. She had come between Karl and his estate foreman then. But surely she wouldn't dare, and had no power to interfere with Adler Classics' employment affairs? No, it couldn't have been from Ilse that the foreman had had his 'orders', and she could think of no one else who had any interest for or against the School, its workers or herself.

She walked into Rutgen at noon, provided by Frau Konstat with a description of the man she hoped might be at the *Wirtshaus*. He was there, drinking a lager at the bar, and though she had expected to have to ask the innkeeper to introduce her, it appeared that he knew her.

He was a chubby, freckled young man with fiery hair. 'Ernst Bürger,' he introduced himself, offering his hand. 'Fräulein Harmon—yes? What may I offer you to drink with me?'

Juliet told him, then said, 'I have to confess I was hoping to meet you, Herr Bürger. Could we move to that table over there?'

'Willingly, Fräulein.'

'Thank you.'

Almost as soon as they were seated she plunged into her subject. He listened, turning his stein between his hands, as, after saying she wouldn't expect an answer to her question if his duty forbade it, she put it to him bluntly——

'Can you tell me, Herr Bürger, by whose orders you rejected all the men who told you they had been skilled wood-carvers at the Schule des Schnitzarbeits, when they applied for jobs with Adler?'

He looked up at her frankly. 'Certainly, Fräulein. I have nothing to hide about that. The order I was given was quite clear—that in no circumstances was my office to entertain any application from any skilled worker lately employed by your School, and it came to me direct from Herr Adler himself.'

Juliet stared, open-mouthed. 'Herr Karl Adler? But that's impossible! He would never have issued any such direction. Besides, he is in hospital, as you know.'

'I had it from him in person,' Ernst Bürger insisted. 'And before the accident on the Klinge ground, of course.'

'When?'

'Last week.'

'Which day, please? Can you remember? It's—important.'

'Tuesday. Yes—Tuesday.'

And it was on the morning of that Tuesday that Karl had scorned the idea that he was in competition with—what had he called the School?—a 'paltry little wood-carving joint'. Later in the same exchange he had taunted her that if she insisted in believing that he had designs on her workers, she could tell herself that he had done no more than act by the rules of the personal war between them—which she had taken as his assumption that, in competition for them or not, she was probably going to lose her workers to him anyway.

So why, after that, had he refused to employ them? What *was* the truth of it all? Could she ... dared she believe, as Magda would have her think, that he had enough pity for her, and enough insight to realise that if he refused employment to her men, they would come back to her? That his move had been another of the few chivalries he had sandwiched between his contempt for and rejection of her—dared she?

But no. There had been no kindness in him when he had flung at her that tag about all being fair in love and war. For when people used it, they were never talking about love. They were only justifying war.

She left Ernst Bürger to his second drink and his *Mittagessen*, no nearer to understanding Karl than she had ever been.

Foreseeing that the men might be embarrassed and humiliated by asking for their jobs back, Juliet approached them herself, claiming that, having heard by a side wind that they hadn't been 'suited' with Adler, she would be greatly obliged if they would consider returning to the School. Increased orders were coming in, (she hadn't got them yet, but she *would*) and she was going to find herself badly in need of their services as before. They fell graciously to the ruse and to a promise of higher pay (Wilhelm's wise advice, this), and returned to their benches to a man.

Magda wrote from Bonn to say that business matters were keeping her away longer than she had expected, and that her return was a little indefinite. News of Karl filtered through from various sources. He had had two major operations on his spine, but nerves had been damaged and there were only guarded hopes of his walking normally again. He would be at the Prinz Franz for some weeks yet, but at his insistence he was managing to conduct some business from his bed.

But none of this came from Ilse Krantz, who hadn't kept her promise to keep Juliet posted, until the day when she did ring up again to say,

'As it occurred to me that you may have heard Karl is allowed some visitors now, and you may have considered going to see him, I thought I should tell you tactfully that you would be wasting your time. Because he has told me in private that he certainly wouldn't welcome you.'

Juliet's breath caught in her throat before she achieved a level, 'I see. But may I ask how it was that my name came up?'

'Quite casually. He was telling me which of his friends and colleagues had been to see him and others that he expected would. I told him the Baronin was still away, but when I mentioned that you might want to thank him for saving that blind boy's life, he said, "Then she can forget it, or save it or thank me by letter if she must. I don't want that girl here." Rather brutally frank of him, I'm afraid,' Ilse concluded blandly.

'But honest at least.'

'Cruel, though. Bitter.'

'And did he ask you to pass on to me what he had said?'

'Not directly. In fact, he may have promised himself the satisfaction of refusing to see you if you did go. No, it was I who thought you ought to be saved the humiliation of that. So I've told you—at the cost of your thinking I'm only making trouble, of course. I didn't like doing it. You do understand that?' Ilse appealed.

'That you had to force yourself? But of *course*!' Juliet echoed, and was rewarded for the hollow triumph of that by Ilse's gasp of righteous indignation before she rang off.

I don't want that girl here. Had she earned such a final rejection by Karl? Juliet wondered. It seemed she had, and she hardly doubted that he had meant it should reach her through Ilse. He had admitted knowing that Ilse disliked her, so he had probably guessed at the zeal with which Ilse would report it. Almost, now and again, she had let herself believe that some time in some vague future she and Karl might reach a kind of accord, or at least a neutrality not too fiercely armed. But—'*I don't want that girl here.*' That finished it. Of his contempt for her, even as an enemy, that said it all—in half a dozen words he had wanted her to hear. He wouldn't willingly meet her again.

As on her earlier return from Bonn, Magda came down to see Juliet, instead of inviting her to the Schloss. She had news, she had announced over the telephone, which she wanted 'Julie' to be the first to hear.

This time it was evident that, whatever her news was, she found it good and too exciting to keep to herself for long after she had arrived. And having prefaced it with the warning, 'Don't you dare say I can't do it!' she brought it out with an air of bravado.

'I am going to take over the management of the hotel again!'

Juliet jerked back her head and frowned, pretending she couldn't believe her ears. 'Say that again,' she demanded mock-sternly. 'I'm not sure that I got it right!'

Magda said it again, and that time Juliet laughed, 'So you did say it and I did hear you, and though it's the very last bit of news I expected, I couldn't, *couldn't* be more glad. You mean that Ilse Krantz——?'

'Will go. She will want a golden handshake, of course, but I am prepared for that, to get the reins back into my own hands.'

'Perhaps,' Juliet suggested, 'she won't expect one, if, as we guessed, she is going to marry Karl Adler when he recovers.'

'Ah, but is she?' Magda questioned.

'She is calling herself his fiancée to people.'

'Not to me. However, I've decided that she and I must part company, in whatever circumstances she goes. For I'm not leaving. And if you are wondering why, less than a year ago, I thought I was too old for it and now have changed my mind, it's because I shan't be carrying the load alone any longer. You don't think me mad, do you?' Magda enquired anxiously.

'Far from it. And you've decided all this while you have been in Bonn?'

'To take on my sister and her husband as partners. As I've told you, he has just retired from the Civil Service where his work was accountancy. So he will see to all the financial business, and my sister and I will share the rest. It was arranging all the technicalities of partnership that kept me away so long, and I couldn't give you a hint by telephone or letter, as *officially* Ilse must be the first to hear of the change. So not a word to anyone yet, Julie, please?'

'You know there won't be,' Juliet assured her. 'But tell me——'

There was so much to tell and discuss, from Magda's alternating euphoria and misgivings, to the practicalities of how and when, that she stayed to supper and for a long time after it. Inevitably at last the talk turned to Karl and to Helmut, who was now at home and working again.

Magda said, not making a question of it, 'And you haven't been to see Karl Adler in the Prinz Franz.'

Juliet shook her head. 'No. But how did you know?'

'Because I have—been to see him, I mean.'

'You have? How? You've been in Bonn!'

'Yes, but on the way back I had a long wait in Munich for my connection to Gutbach, where my car was meeting me. So I went to the hospital and was allowed a little time with him.'

'How—was he?'

'Himself. Thinner. Rather drawn, from all he has been through. But thinking forward. Seeing a future ahead now.'

'He couldn't at first?' Juliet questioned.

'He says not. At first he was all despair, until they let him try to walk again, and he could, though of course only limping with a stick. But I think you should have visited him in all this while, Julie. I know how he affects you, but wouldn't it have been a courtesy at least?'

Juliet looked away. 'He hasn't wanted to see me,' she said.

'What makes you think so?'

'He told Ilse. She passed on the message, and considering how he and I last parted—by telephone—I wasn't surprised.'

Magda sighed. 'Oh dear, what is it between you two? So what happened over the telephone?'

'I accused him of tempting away my workers with his offer of fantastic wages. He claimed Adler Classics wouldn't stoop to competing with the likes of me, but when he said I must realise that all was fair in love and war, I took that as an admission that he had coaxed them away. But then a rather strange thing happened——'

'What?' asked Magda patiently.

'Well, when the men were free of their notice to me,

and they applied for the jobs, the pay foreman said he had orders not to take them on, and now they are reasonably happily back with me.'

'And doesn't that show that you had accused Karl wrongly?'

Juliet frowned in perplexity. 'I don't know. I don't know what to think. If he hadn't said that about love and war——'

'But a lot has happened for Karl since then,' Magda reminded her. 'For one thing, he has risked his life for poor Helmut Jäger. And as soon as you heard his friends could visit him, weren't you ever tempted to put matters straight between you over something so trivial and behind you? *Weren't* you, Julie—ever?'

'Not when he had told Isle he wouldn't see me.'

'Though if you hadn't heard that, would you have swallowed your pride and gone to see him?'

'I don't know. I don't think so.'

Magda sighed again. 'I'm sorry. I'd have given a great deal to hear you say Yes,' she said.

'Would you?' Juliet waited for Magda to tell her why—in vain. Magda had no more to say. But though Juliet knew her friend did not mean her silence as a rebuke, she could not help wishing that just for once Magda would urge, persuade, even goad. It was not her way, as Juliet had always known and appreciated, but this time, when it would have taken so little— pitifully little!—Dutch courage to send her running to Karl to say 'I'm sorry' or whatever less or more he would listen to—— She felt, however unfairly, that Magda had let her down. If Magda had told her she must go to him, she would have gone.

It could hardly be said that Rutgen was electrified by

the news that the Baronin meant to resume management of the hotel. The Lake folk did not frequent it themselves. The village *Wirtshaus* was their favoured hostelry, and the departure or supplanting of mine host, Herr Munster, and his good lady would have caused a good deal more stir.

Juliet had dreaded for Magda her difficult interview with Ilse. But apparently Ilse took the news of her replacement with haughty calm, claiming only that she wasn't too sorry; she had never had great hopes of detaching the hotel from its previous dowdy image except in the long term, and in the short term she had, in any case, other plans which might have necessitated the breaking of her contract herself.

'She still hasn't mentioned any engagement to me, and she may have been making the best of sour grapes,' Magda reported. 'But I suppose one must conclude that her "other plans" mean that she is going to marry Karl Adler. Though I hope not, and when I go to see him again, I shall be rude enough to ask him, I think. Perhaps only to hear the worst—that when he has built his house on the Fichte Platte I shall have seen the last of Ilse here at the Schloss, only to have her as a neighbour, which prospect I do *not* welcome at all.'

Not a word nor a question from Magda as to whether Juliet had had second thoughts about visiting Karl herself. As always, Magda was standing off from any persuasion or dictation, and even when, a few days later, she rang to ask that Juliet should do her the favour of delivering to the hospital some books which she had promised to Karl, she emphasised that Juliet need only leave them with one of the nurses. She herself had taken to her bed with a heavy chill, but she would send the books down to Juliet by her driver.

For Juliet it was an errand without overtones of ruse on Magda's part. All Magda had asked was that she should deliver the parcel to Karl's ward, and that was what she was going to do—leave it and come away.

But she was to find the ward in a state of high crisis. While she waited on the corridor three or four patients' trolleys were wheeled quickly past her and into the ward, without a glance or a word being thrown her way. Nurses with preoccupation written on their faces came and went; the lift doors opened and shut on white-coated housemen bound to or from the ward, and it was some time before Juliet managed to corner a staff nurse to give her message and to proffer the books.

The harassed girl fingered her waistband instead of taking them. 'Look,' she confided, 'we've a terrible flap on—an autobahn accident, and we're just getting the intake up from Casualty. Sister is off duty and—well, why not take the stuff in to Herr Adler yourself? There are no restrictions on his visits now, and that's his door there, though he may be out on his balcony—— Yes, Nurse—coming!' She withdrew her attention from Juliet to answer a junior signalling to her from a doorway, and the next minute she was gone.

Juliet hesitated, her heart quickening its beat almost painfully. Should she? Dared she? What would Karl say when she told him she was acting messenger for the Baronin who was ill? He would have to say something, if only to thank her for the books or to enquire for Magda. He couldn't just ignore her, look *through* her —could he?

She moved like an automaton towards his door. Until she touched its handle she could always turn

back ... But as soon as she turned it her resolve
hardened. She would take what was coming to her—
whatever was. And she longed to see him so *much*.

His room was airy, sunny and empty, the bed neat,
the stretch of the polished floor a small desert to be
crossed to the open french window and the minute
balcony beyond. Juliet stepped out on to it, close to
the head of the chaise-longue which stood there; the
figure lying on it neither roused nor even stirred.

She had surprised Karl deeply asleep, as he had once
surprised her. Very softly she moved forward a few
steps, to stand by his side, looking down at him. There
was a light woollen rug over his knees and thighs; his
cap-sleeved shirt was open to its lower buttons and he
had lost little if any of his deep tan. Asleep and as
defenceless as she remembered he had claimed to find
her, he was younger than his years, one of the golden
lads of Shakespeare's lyric, and as she yearned for him
every nerve ached to dare as he had done to her—to
kiss, just once, without his waking.

Not his lips. That was too dangerous. His hand
which drooped to the floor, palm open and upturned?
Or the long exposed line of his collarbone which had
fascinated her once before? Though she knew it was
impossible, tempted, she dropped silently to her knees
and bent over him. As long as she didn't touch him, he
wouldn't ever know.

But her breath must have feather-touched his bare
skin, for he stirred, arched his spine, and though his
eyes remained closed his arms went round her, drawing her so close that her face was pressed into the
hollow of his shoulder. Held so, she could not see
whether he had wakened enough to know what he was
doing or who she was, until one of his hands went

gropingly to her hair and the other slackened its pressure on her back.

Freed, she lifted her head—to meet the aware, searching look in his blue eyes—and had a moment's panic thought, *So he is conscious. He does know*, before his parted lips came down in hungry, demanding possession of her mouth and, her control no match for her own desire, she became all response, all yielding, all surrender ... giving and taking, not questioning nor rejecting in those moments of recognition of and pity for the male need which spoke in every sensual kiss and every caressing movement of his restless hands.

For he wasn't making love to her. He was long-deprived Male seeking physical solace of Female; in that need the seductive touch of any woman-flesh would serve him well, and that she could forgive and understand. She had been able to give him some measure of release, and for the moment her love asked no more.

He calmed, and she came to her feet slowly, expecting no apology and getting none. He said roughly, 'I suppose Magda von Boden sent you, and obediently you came?'

She nodded. 'Yes.'

His lip curled. 'I thought as much. She may have had to twist your arm, but with teeth set and dogged in the face of duty, you came.'

Puzzled, Juliet said, 'Magda only wanted me to bring some books—those,' indicating them with a finger—'but she didn't ask me to see you; just to leave them on the ward for you.'

'Indeed? And why didn't you?'

'Because they've an emergency on and had no time

for me. A staff nurse asked me to deliver them myself, and so I did.'

'Nobly ignoring the risk you might be running, but finding me asleep, deciding you might as well inspect the damaged goods while you were here?'

She felt hot colour flood her face. 'Risk? What risk?' she asked.

'Of having to make a show of a sympathy you couldn't feel; the kind of compassion you didn't afford to Gerhard's infirmities and which you couldn't drum up for me. So you took a furtive look and even knelt for a closer inspection. Not much to see, though, is there?' With an irritable flick of finger and thumb he threw back the covering rug. 'Look, two legs still, two thighs, a wonky spine which doesn't show. I shall crawl in time, even if I can't run. Satisfied now that you don't have to go through the motions of squeezing out any pity for me? But for God's sake, woman,' he suddenly exploded, 'didn't Ilse tell you that I didn't want you here, wouldn't see you if you came?'

Juliet flinched from his vehemence. Through dry lips she said, 'Yes, she told me, and I shouldn't have come now if Magda had expected I should have to see you.' She paused and regaining some spirit, demanded, 'But why me? You've been seeing Ilse Krantz—naturally. And I think you welcomed Magda, and there must have been plenty of your friends whom you've seen. So why not me? Haven't I the right to know?'

He scanned her face thoughtfully. Then his eyes dropped in deliberate appraisal of her figure, the jut of her hips revealed by the lines of her low-cut summer dress. She might have been something inanimate he was deciding whether or not to buy. Raising his eyes again, '*Don't* you know?' he asked.

'No.'

'Then your own comparison with Ilse and the
Baronin should tell you. It's because neither they nor
anyone else I know have your hang-ups in the face of
a man's inadequacy; your impatience of it, your
ostensible ability to pity—but only so long as pity asks
nothing of you. Make myself clear, do I, as to why I
told Ilse that if you dared to come, I'd throw you out?'

Listening, appalled, Juliet felt almost physically
sick. With a hand to her throat, she whispered, 'Very
clear. Very, very clear. You thought *that* of me? That
I couldn't admire you, or be grateful to you for
Helmut's sake, or—care that you——?' Unable to go
on, she could only stare dumbly, biting her lip to stop
its trembling.

Karl said, 'Gratitude, admiration, concern—oh,
you'd have worn them all right, I daresay. It's just that
I wasn't prepared to witness a performance which
would probably have been about as phoney as your
co-operation just now. Superbly done, I'll admit. But
phoney it had to be.'

Her tone still scarcely audible, she said, 'It wasn't
phoney. I wasn't putting on an act, I—I understood——'

'Understood? Understood what?' he barked.

How could she express her instinctive sensing of his
need? But he was waiting, and she had to try. 'I meant
that I realised ... understood that it wasn't me you
were making love to. *As* me, that is—— But I just
happened to be there, when it might have been almost
anyone else. You weren't wanting me, or asking me to
want you—— It was your reaction to finding me near
to you when you woke, and I—sort of—wanted to

help. Oh, do try to understand what I mean!' she appealed.

She shrank from the glint of anger in his eyes. 'I don't have to try too hard,' he said. 'You found me so sex-starved that if it had been Anna the ward maid or Kirsty the newspaper girl whom I'd found hovering when I woke, I'd have clinched with either of them just for the hell of it, as readily as I did with you. Is that what you're saying? *Is* it?'

She nodded reluctantly. 'I suppose so. I only know that it wasn't me you wanted in your arms. It couldn't have been.'

'Any more than your response was anything but kindness, "wanting to help"? As you've admitted, you were kindness itself to Gerhard until he asked too much.' Suddenly, though with some difficulty, Karl hunched himself round to lie on one hip with his back to her. Over his shoulder he said wearily, 'Oh, go away. You and I get nowhere with words, and we've already spent a lot too many doing it. So go away please—now.'

'Very well.' She turned, but as she reached the door he spoke again.

'Of course you could ask yourself why, both Anna and Kirsty being pretty wenches and as far as I know uncommitted and probably willing, I should have managed to control my baser urges until you came along and "happened" to be there when I had to pounce. But if you do come up with an answer, don't bother to tell me. For I really couldn't care less.'

CHAPTER TEN

AUTUMN came early but gently to the Silbersee. September was barely in before there was a bite of dawn frost in the air; sometimes rime made white lace of every spider web in the hedgerows, and the falling leaves, richly red and gold before they fell, dried and browned into a brittle crackle of carpet for the forest floor.

But that year there were no storms to lash the lake to fury, and the fogs which hid the towering Volksspitze and its sister peaks would usually clear by noon, drifting away, wisp by wisp, leaving behind a short but warm golden day.

There were still some summer tourists at the hotel. Magda's relatives had settled in as her co-managers, and it was regaining the image she had wanted for it. It had lost a certain clientèle with Ilse's departure, but it was attracting another, and Magda claimed that at least now she hadn't to shut her eyes to garishness every time she walked through its public rooms.

Ilse had left without demanding a too-heavy compensation, saying magnanimously that even trying to pull into shape a hopeless proposition like the Schloss when she had come to it could be counted as experience by which she might profit if she should consider embarking on anything similar in the future. Whereat she disappeared, though whether back into Munich society or to a wider field, no one heard. For Karl, after leaving the hospital for convalescence in a local nursing-home, had also left the region, his return understood to be indefinite. He could walk with a slight

limp and he could drive his car. He was making a
leisurely tour of the Italian Lakes, it was said. But
whether Ilse was with him or was meeting him, either
no one of his colleagues knew, or they were not saying.

The sawmill on the Klinge Platte had gone up at
incredible speed, and on these still days the hum of its
machinery made a kind of muted backing to all the
other lake sounds—the shouts of the timbermen, the
swish-swish of the water displaced by the launches, the
bickering of the birds and the noise of the trundling
lorries on the rough estate roads. It was an intrusive
sound, but it wasn't offensive, and even Juliet had to
admit that she would miss it if it weren't there.

Since that humiliating and heart-tearing parting
from Karl, she had put every mental and physical
power she had into work, to save herself from thinking
... remembering. She *thought* wood-carving, dreamed
it, sold it, and when she failed to sell it, plugged on
until she did. She was lucky. These late summer weeks
were the buyers' ordering season for their Christmas
trade. The School gradually had as much work as it
could handle. Juliet cut expenses mercilessly and paid
out bonuses on total sales. So far at least she felt she
had paid her debt to Gerhard. She had saved his
School. Saved it at a cost which no one but she would
ever know, but *saved* it.

Sunday. The warmth of the sun already peeling the
mist from the mountain-tops and from the lake surface.
The gay tunes of the church bells' weekday *Glockenspiel* sobered to a single chime for Sundays. Everyone
gathered on the Square or on the church steps, waiting
for the dying of the last peal which would signal the
concerted trooping into church. A typical Rutgen
Sunday ritual, centuries old. Greeting and being

greeted by her neighbours as they came out again at noon, Juliet felt she could be completely content with their little world which she had made her own, if it were not for the dull ache of the heart-hunger which never fully lifted from her spirit.

From the dim light of the church to the glare outside was a contrast which called for sunglasses. Taking hers from her bag and adjusting them, she lingered on the steps for a few minutes, watching the boys and girls scuttling to their machines, mounting them and cur- vetting round the Square and away towards the heights, exhausts snorting and engines on full power. That left the Square's parking empty except for one or two cars of uncertain age and—one other, the sight and recognition of which sent Juliet's pulses racing.

Karl's car! And that was Karl alighting from it. Karl, walking tall, and except for the stick on which he hardly seemed to rely, walking over to her with much the same confidence as he had done all those months ago on the Innsgort road. The few people still gossip- ing at the foot of the church steps recognised him too, and he saluted them with his stick. But he came straight on to face Juliet. 'Magda told me I should find you here,' he said.

She took off her glasses and fingered them nerv- ously. 'Yes. I usually come—— You—wanted to see me about something?' she hesitated.

'Wanted to see you,' he said, making it sound so like a correction that she sent a puzzled glance at the blue eyes made level with her own by his stance on the step lower than hers. 'To see you,' his emphasis answered the glance, and then with an irrelevance which startled her, 'are you hungry?' he asked.

'Hungry? Why, no——'

'Good. For we aren't picnicking this time. Later, perhaps.' His hand invited her down the steps, and she went with him and across the Square, dumb with wonder that he should want to take her anywhere, if he only meant to drive her back to the School. She let him put her into the car. Discarding his stick, he took his own seat. 'Where are we going?' she asked.

'Up. You'll see.' Driving with the consummate ease he had always done, Karl swung round the Square and out on to the forest road in the wake of the mopeds and motor-cycles now far ahead of them. As if they had taken an agreed vow of silence neither Juliet nor he spoke again while the car climbed the winding road—not to the Schloss, she realised, but higher. Where then? To the Fichte Platte? To the thought which had asked the question a sudden gleam of intuition was able to answer Yes. But *why*? What could he want of her there? Neither thought nor intuition had an answer to that.

The branching cart-track up to the little plateau was broader now, smooth as a private drive. The car purred up it, instead of rocking from one rut to the next, and Karl drew up on a scene which wasn't a total surprise to Juliet.

She had heard that the house he had planned for himself had been a-building in his absence, but she had never been tempted to go again to watch the progress of the home he was probably building for Ilse Krantz to share. Yet here it was, its form and area roughly defined, though only by its metre-high walls as yet. The springy sward all round it was a mess of builders' rubble, and lorries were parked under the trees where she had lunched with Karl's architect, when Karl had been as caustic with him as he had

been with her—as usual. But there had been no unnecessary butchery of the surrounding trees, and she
noticed with jealous gratification that the house was
going to face the way her imagination had planned it
should. Again she asked herself why he had brought
her to see it. Could be it was his idea of revenge—
showing her that for as long as she stayed on the Lake,
he would be an ever-present threat to her peace of
mind when he lived here? But surely even he couldn't
be as cruel as that? And somehow the look which had
met hers on the church steps hadn't glinted with its
usual warning of trouble to come. It had been frank
and bland enough to flood her with the wild hope that
he did want to see her because—well, because he
wanted to, that was all.

In order to look across at the house she had turned
sideways. Karl had turned slightly too, one arm
crooked on the steering wheel, the other across the
back of her seat, the fingers of that hand playing an idle
tattoo within an inch or two of her shoulder. 'Well,' he
said, 'what do you think of it?'

What was there to 'think' of a skeleton, except of its
promise when it was clothed? Juliet said, 'It's a lovely
site, and you're going to have a breathtaking view.
When do you expect it to be finished?'

'In about eight or nine months—about the best time
for getting a sale, the early summer.'

'A sale?' She looked sharply back at him. 'But Herr
—I forget his name—told me you were building it for
yourself!'

'That was the original idea, but I've had reason and
time enough to doubt my hopes of it since. It may be
that I've wantonly destroyed them myself. But if I

have, I want out from the place, and the first bidder
for it can have it.'

Was he telling her that his engagement to Ilse had
fallen through? But why bring her here, only to be so
cryptic about it? And did he consciously realise, Juliet
wondered, that the mute tune made by his fingers on
the leather of her seat was now being played as lightly
on her upper arm? Though not caring, of course, if he
did know he was doing it, how her imagination longed
to turn even so idle a contact into a caress.

She was at a loss for a reply to his bitterness. If he
did mean he had broken with Isle, or she with him,
she couldn't in honesty tell him she was sorry. For she
wouldn't be. She managed instead, 'I hope you won't
abandon the plans you had for the house. Or have you
decided against them already?'

The absent drumming on her arm stopped. 'Not entirely yet. In certain circumstances I might change my
mind,' he said, sending her spirits plunging at the
implication that his break with Ilse wasn't final.

He was opening both doors of the car. 'Let's get out,
shall we? I'd appreciate your opinion on the layout of
the rooms, so far as I understand it.'

Side by side they walked over to the foundations.
There Juliet halted and looked up at him. 'Why?' she
asked bluntly. 'Why my opinion? Why should you
want it?'

'Why not?' he countered. 'Didn't architect Brentl
claim that you'd shown some expertise in design? If I
remember, you denied me a share in your ideas at the
time, but if you could see your way to being a little
more generous now——?' he invited, in his tone the
same taunting note which had always been a tinder for
the flame of her rancour. So here they were again, look-

ing for vulnerable spots in which to place their barbs!

She said, 'You were laughing at me then—you both were—and if you can't think of a better reason for asking what my opinion is now, then I'd be very grateful if you would drive me home.'

'Before I've told you why I wanted to see you?'

'Well, haven't you? Pretending you want my interest in a house in which you admit you may already have lost your own!'

'Implying that you could drum up some enthusiasm for it, only if I showed some myself?'

'I didn't say that——!'

'No.' He paused, then added incredibly, 'Though I could wish you had.'

'Why?'

He sighed. 'How you overwork that word!'

Driven to desperation, Juliet turned on him. 'Only because I don't understand anything that's going on; your reason for bringing me here; your claim just now that you care whether or not I like the house. Just as if you could!' she jeered.

His steady eyes held hers. 'I did tell you that, given certain factors, my own faith in it might well take new heart,' he reminded her.

'So you did. But factors—such as?'

'That you should care about it too, want to watch it taking shape, look forward to enjoying it. Which would make two of us of the same mind,' he said.

That was so bizarre that it asked to be laughed to scorn. So she laughed without mirth or warmth. 'You and I—of one mind about *anything*? Ever? You hate me. You despise me—you've shown me that in more ways than one. You set out to destroy me because the School was in your way. You told Ilse Krantz that if

I tried to see you at the Prinz Franz you would throw me out, and when I did come—by accident!—you did just that. And now you dare——!' She broke off, fretted by pain.

She had to wait for his reply. When it came, 'And nothing about my rejecting you dovetails in your mind with what I'm trying to tell you now?' he questioned. '*Mein Gott*, woman'—with one hand he spun her about and so close to him that his face was out of focus to her bewitched stare—'have you no conception of what it meant to me to realise that I might be only half a man for the rest of my days? For I had Gerhard as a warning, hadn't I? *He* was broken, useless, as I might be. He had loved you, as I did and do. So do you wonder that I drew parallels? That I couldn't bear to see your face or listen to your sympathy, or suffer your "kindness"? *Do* you?'

Miracle or mirage—which? 'Love me?' Juliet echoed. 'Love *me*? How can you? Or claim that I ought to know it? You've never let me guess, nor shown me——'

'There've been occasions when I've tried,' he said quietly.

She coloured hotly, remembering the cavalier way in which he had kissed her awake in his car, the later savagery with which he had forced the surrender of her lips in a storm of passion, but a passion of anger, not of love; avenging Gerhard, he had claimed. Both times, though he did not know it, he had had all her willingness, all her woman's answer, but each time he had ravished without giving anything of himself in return. And his spurning of her when she had knelt beside him—there again he seemed now to be asking her to believe that the reverse side of his repulse of her was a love which had been too proud to parley for hers. What was the truth? Would he have told her he loved her if he did not? Would he have *dared*?

She said slowly, 'If you have wanted me to know, I've never understood——'

'Nor wanted to?' The stick slung over his wrist slipped to the ground unheeded, and his arms went round her. '*Nor wanted to?*' he urged again.

In some odd way the very rawness of the despair in his voice seemed to be the measure of a hope he hardly dared sustain. Juliet lifted her head and leaned back against the bulwark of his arms. 'Wanted to—for a very long time,' she whispered. 'Hadn't you known either?'

He shook his head slowly in doubt. 'If you had only ever let me guess! But you are saying it now, my sweet? Meaning it? That you love me ... want me, as I want you?'

Her answer was to draw his face down to hers and to kiss his lips. At which, with an 'A-a-h!' of incredulous wonder, his desire seemed to catch fire, his hands and his mouth touching and exploring, his eyes alight with worship, his body seeking to mould the soft pliancy of hers to the whole vital line of his own; quickening her blood to a wild abandon as hot and passion-urged as his.

This she had asked of him for far too long, and this he had always withheld until now. For this wasn't a brutal demand for her surrender. In turn this was a gentle search for her willingness, and a heady storm of rapturous ecstasy from which neither was asking nor granting shelter; they were at one with it, allowing it to toss them to the heights together and finding the calm of tenderness when it had passed. This was needing, giving, belonging—and yet, after a timelessness which wasn't to be counted by the clock, for Juliet a shadow fell. There could be no belonging to Karl until——

She forced herself to draw back from him and to his questioning look she named the shadow. 'Gerhard,' she said.

Karl understood. 'Yes, Gerhard,' he said. And then, 'I don't think you'll ever realise how badly I wanted at first to punish you over him.'

'You did punish me, and made very sure that I knew what the punishment was for.'

He nodded. 'That night on the launch I'd let jealousy convince me that you were at much the same thing again with young Seiber—leading him on and holding aloof when he overstepped your Keep Out signs and claimed what he expected were his rights. You would have let Gerhard follow the same path, I decided, before you turned him down, and I confess I meant to hurt you where I thought it would wound you most—in your frigid self-conceit.'

Juliet flinched. 'And yet that same night you took the trouble to see me safe from Johan Seiber.'

'Yes, and it was always like that—I've been for ever swinging between contempt of you and admiration of your courage; between hating the image which you seemed determined to defend at the cost of any regard I had for you, and softening to you and loving you to distraction. The loving won——'

'In spite of Gerhard?'

'Rather because of him. Because when I knew I loved you, I began—though only slowly—to be grateful that your history with regard to him had been what it was; grateful that you hadn't loved him, or married him for less that the love *I* wanted of you. From there I could argue that you had been right, and since I've been travelling during these weeks—literally miles, and on an even longer journey in my mind towards the hope of you—I've prayed more than once that Gerhard knows now that you would have wronged him if you had married him for pity, and that he may forgive us both.'

Juliet said, 'This could be wishful thinking, but I believe he had always loved the School more than he loved me. I was only a late figure on his scene; the School was his life. I couldn't love him, but I felt I did owe it to him to keep it going, which is why I've fought you over it as I have.'

Karl's mouth lifted in a half-smile. 'And how you've fought me, *mein Liebchen*!'

'Fought your threats against it!'

'And how many of them have I carried out?'

'You *made* them.'

'And at first meant every word of them. Juliet Harmon and her Schule des Schnitzarbeits, making carved piggy-banks and fretwork fern-holders, were going to be bought out or winkled out before they realised what had hit them. But once I began to enjoy the in-fighting with you, I wanted to keep it going. And once I knew I loved you, my plans went out of the window, and I had to keep you there.'

'By persuading your business friends to give me orders? Didn't you know how I should resent that?'

'And did you expect me to watch you drop out of the rat-race for want of a bit of encouragement?'

'I've managed without it alone since then,' she claimed proudly. 'Now, we are getting all the work the School can handle.' She moved closer again to trace the line of his jacket lapel with an idle finger as she added, 'But that's something I've never understood. How kind you could sometimes be, and how your threats and your actions didn't always add up. I thought——'

'You thought me vindictive over your gleaning rights, for instance?'

'And then found you weren't.'

'And that I was outpricing you in the labour market?'

'Until your pay foreman told me he had your orders not to take on any of my people. But before I could apologise to you about that, you——' She stopped, wincing from the memory of the happenings of an afternoon which still haunted her dreams.

Karl drew her to him again. 'Yes, all right,' he said. 'I meanly bowed out from our private battlefield, just in time to thwart your donning your sackcloth and ashes—is that it?'

'I'd still have come to you wearing them, if you hadn't refused to see me.'

'My heart, I've already told you why not!'

'And I—well, I lied when I said I hadn't meant to try to see you. As soon as I was tempted, I did.'

'And knelt by me for some dire purpose of your own—not wholly by chance?' he teased.

'I was longing to kiss you while you were asleep, but knowing you were sure to wake, I daren't.'

'I wasn't asleep. I'd seen you kneel. But when I kissed you—you!—*you*, only you, I sensed your heart wasn't in it, and later you had to admit as much— you'd been feeding my long need to make love to a woman, that was all, you implied.'

'I had to. You'd been so passionate, and—so had I, that I dared not delude myself that you were making love to me. There was Ilse. You were engaged to her.'

'That was a very long time ago. Before she married someone else.'

'You kept her portrait on your desk. I saw it there.'

'She expected to see it when she came to my apartment. She knew the camera had etherealised her, made her more seductive than she was, and it didn't cost much to indulge her vanity. What's more, knowing you would have seen the photograph, I argued that a little competition would do you no harm.'

'Ilse claims to be your fiancée still.'

'Ex only——'

'No. It privileged her to see you when the hospital wouldn't have let me.'

'Then there's why she claimed it. It was a score over you. But here——' releasing Juliet, he reached into a pocket for a newspaper cutting. 'From a gossip column in a Florida paper—you see, Ilse on the arm of her second husband, a lately acquired property tycoon. Does that convince you that she and I are now not even "good friends"?'

Juliet looked at Ilse's self-congratulatory face, read the caption of the picture, handed back the cutting. 'You said once that you could guess why she didn't like me. What did you mean?'

'I sensed that she had been jealous of you all along.'

'Magda thought you were going to marry her.'

He shook his head. 'Not now, if she ever did. Your Magda von Boden is a wise, wise woman, and Ilse was equally acute to danger.'

'Danger?' queried Juliet.

'That what has happened for you and me might be going to happen. As it has, hasn't it, sweetheart?' he pleaded. Tell me again. Show me——'

There was so much more to say, to tell, to ask. But there would be time for that. Now they shared the primitive urge implanted by insatiable Nature—the need to touch and to look, their desirous bodies yearning to be generous of passion; his dominant, demanding, hers vibrant with response. While they clung together the eloquence of their embrace was its own love-language. They had no need of speech, and when at last they drew apart, all their mental barriers were down, destroyed by their new understanding that though the needs and motives and reactions of each might differ they would always be resolved in the total handfast oneness of their mating.

Juliet giggled shyly, 'You were going to show me the house.'

'Then come along.' He led her through the rubble to the rudiments of an entrance. 'The front door. Don't trip over the mat. This spacious rectangle—the salon; this lesser square, the dining-room. This—a summer breakfast-room opening on to what will be our garden. Note the tasteful rockwork. Kitchen and "usual offices"——' He cocked a mischievous blue eye. 'Just as well perhaps that there's no first floor as yet, hm?'

' "As well"?'

'Because if there were a master bedroom, who can tell how I might be tempted? I should carry you bodily across the threshold and——'

She played along. 'I'd always understood you did that at the front door?'

'I shall create a precedent by doing it at both,' he claimed. 'When are you going to marry me?'

'You can't carry a bride across a threshold, let alone

two, until you've got a threshold to carry her across,' she pointed out.

'True. But in this case the order has to be—bride first, threshold second. So when?'

They sat side by side on a slab of coping stone, talking, teasing and making plans.

Karl said, 'Magda sent me to you this morning, more or less on pain of execution if I didn't come back engaged to you.'

Juliet laughed happily. 'I believe she has always wanted to sell you to me.'

'But you weren't buying?'

'I was—if I'd had that much treasure to spend, but I hadn't. You weren't for me, I was sure.'

Later she ventured, 'The School—I'd like it to go on.'

'Meaning you want to carry it on?'

'If you agree. If you'd let me.'

'Ah.' Karl made of his frown a thunderous menace. 'I should need notice of that question. Notice—and a timetable of when I can spare you duly drawn up,' he threatened.

Juliet took his hand, turned it palm upward and dropped a kiss there. 'I hope you'll never really *want* to spare me,' she murmured.

'Never, dearest heart—from now till infinity,' he said.

And there's still *more* love in

Yes!

Four more spellbinding
romantic stories every month
by your favorite authors.
Elegant and sophisticated tales of
love and love's conflicts.

Let your imagination be swept away to
exotic places in search of adventure,
intrigue and romance. Get to
know the warm, true-to-life
characters. Share the special
kind of miracle that
love can be.

Don't miss out. Buy now and discover
the world of HARLEQUIN PRESENTS...

Do you have a favorite
Harlequin author?
Then here is an
opportunity you must
not miss!

HARLEQUIN OMNIBUS

Each volume contains
3 full-length compelling
romances by one author.
Almost 600 pages of
the very best in romantic
fiction for only $2.75

A wonderful way to collect
the novels by the Harlequin
writers you love best!

What the press says about Harlequin Romances...

"...clean, wholesome fiction...always with an upbeat, happy ending."
— *San Francisco Chronicle*

"...a work of art."
— *The Globe & Mail*, Toronto

"Nothing quite like it has happened since *Gone With the Wind*..."
— *Los Angeles Times*

"...among the top ten..."
— *International Herald-Tribune*, Paris

"The most popular reading matter of
American women today."
— *The Detroit News*

"Women have come to trust these
clean easy-to-read stories about
contemporary people, set in exciting
foreign places."
— *Best Sellers*, New York

"Harlequin novels have a vast and
loyal readership."
— *Toronto Star*

What readers say about Harlequin Romances

"Your books are the best I have ever found."
P.B.* Bellevue. Washington

"I enjoy them more and more
with each passing year."
J.L. Spurlockville. West Virginia

"No matter how full and happy life might be,
it is an enchantment to sit
and read your novels."
D.K. Willowdale. Ontario

"I firmly believe that Harlequin Romances
are perfect for anyone who wants to read
a good romance."
C.R. Akron. Ohio

*Names available on request